Praise for *Icarus Never Flew 'Round Here*

"Dale makes for an authentically frightening figure... His descent into madness is a quiet, slow burn. The narrative skillfully portrays a man who never seems to flinch."

—*Kirkus Reviews*

"Although Edwards deals with vast ideas, his attention to detail, especially in regards to place and dialect, brings a specificity to the world of the novel. The tone is always beautifully set."

—Madeline Barbush, *Independent Book Review*

"A literary reflection on the affects of isolation, theological examination, and one soul's descent that offers a thought-provoking read that surprises on many different levels."

—D. Donovan, Senior Reviewer, *Midwest Book Review*

"[Edwards] has written a novel that is bound to pique readers' curiosity and leave them thinking about things long after they put the book down."

—*Literary Titan*

"Matt Edwards' smooth prose and addictive narrative keep their hold on you from start to finish. This is a riveting story that follows a man's slow descent into madness as he buries himself in the rabbit hole of trying to discern meaning from events way above his station."

—Pikasho Deka, *Readers' Favorite*

D1564996

ICARUS NEVER FLEW 'ROUND HERE

A NOVEL

MATT EDWARDS

atmosphere press

Published by Atmosphere Press

Cover design by Matthew Fielder

atmospherepress.com

For Marianna, Elia, and the very first readers of *Ways and Truths and Lives*

If emotion can create a physical action, then duplicating the physical action can re-create the emotion.

— Chuck Palahniuk, *Diary*

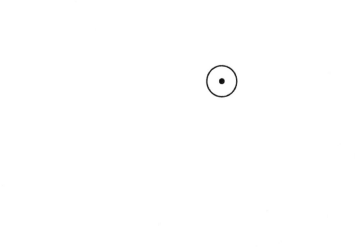

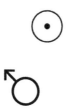

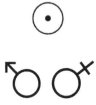

"Or so it goes."

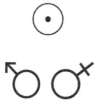

HORIZON

Dale thrusts the posthole digger into the shallow soil. The impact of hitting yet another rock reverberates through his hands, arms, and shoulders. He pulls the handles apart, and the blades scrape together more of the earth. Looking up through parted hands, he notices the sky salted with clouds stretching all the way to the horizon. He pauses, focusing on a fixed point between land and sky. The inconstant, white forms float by in a languid current; Earth's rotation appears momentarily tangible.

"Whatta ya want from me?" Dale asks. "I know yur out there." He lifts the dirt out and dumps it in a pile. "Ya got nothin' better ta do?" He kneels next to the hole and reaches down its full two feet to extract a rock. With a little jolt and shimmy, it comes loose. "Is this what ya want?" Dale says, gesturing at the horizon line with the rock in his hand. "Nah, of course not." And with that, the rock plops down onto a small mound of dirt.

Dale continues to dig.

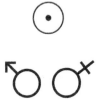

FENCES

Dale's boots hammer the length of the front porch, knocking off all excess dirt. His hands vigorously slap wispy brown clouds out from the front of his pants and shirt. The screen door snaps shut.

"How's the new fence comin'?" Janice asks, pulling potatoes out of the oven.

"It's comin'." Dale hangs his hat on a cast-iron wall hook.

"Ya sure yur not just workin' yurself ragged? I know that's not easy diggin'." Janice shakes her hands free of her paisley oven mitts.

"I don't mind."

"Well, that's what ya say, but—"

"I thought I told ya not ta use the oven when it's this hot out," Dale barks.

"Ya did. But ya also told me ya like yur potatoes cooked and not raw, so pick yur poison," Janice retorts with out-turned fists on her hips.

"Alright, let's not get started—"

"Besides, we were talkin' about the new fence."

"What about it?" Dale slides back a chair and sits himself at the table.

"Well, I just think yur wastin' yur time. The old fence still looks perfectly fine." Janice turns her attention to a bowl of salad.

"Lots of thangs look fine from inside yur comfy house. But I'm not gonna sit around like some people and wait for the thang ta fall ta pieces. It's time for a new fence, so I'm puttin' in a new fence."

"Fine, fine, fine. Have it yur way. Do ya have anythang ta drink?"

"Water's fine."

"Well, can't ya see I'm busy?" Janice says, waving a pair of wooden salad tongs.

"I'll get it." Dale stands up and limps into the kitchen.

"Wash yur hands while yur over there. Dinner's ready."

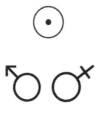

USE

The dirt trickles in around the new cedar fence post as Dale's shovel avoids all sizable rocks until the hole is nearly filled. As he scrapes the ground flush with the edge of his shovel, something catches his eye amongst the scattered rocks. He toes it with the shovel blade. Its weight and consistency are different from the other rocks. He crouches down to take a closer look. Its color is essentially that of the rocks, but its shape is much more uniform and exact. He fingers it back and forth. Dale looks over his shoulder and sees Amelia, his one and only Red Poll, staring at him, a mere ten feet away.

"What?"

Amelia continues to stare. Turning back around, Dale decides to pick up the mysterious object. It is light in his hands, and as he turns the turnip-shaped object over and over, Dale notices a small opening, previously caked with dirt, revealing the object to be hollow.

"What are *you*?" Dale asks, then pauses to look back over his shoulder at Amelia. "Mind yur own business."

Dale hurriedly scatters the remaining rocks around the base of the fence post, gets up, and marches toward the house.

* * *

"Whatta ya make a this?" Dale asks, the small turnip-shaped thing resting in the palm of his hand.

Janice looks up from the pages of *Jane Eyre,* basking in the remnants of the late morning sun, and turns in her armchair to squint at the object. "What is it?"

"I don't know. That's what I'm askin' *you.*" Dale shoves his hand closer to Janice's face. Her eyes scan back and forth.

"It sure looks like somethin', though, donit?"

"Yeah, I'm thinkin' it's Indian."

"What makes ya say that?"

"Well, it looks old, first of all. I was also noticin' these smudges. It looks like it was painted. See those li'l pictures?" Dale runs his finger across the object's belly.

"Oh, yeah." Janice cranes her neck forward, her chin almost touching Dale's fingertips. "Whatta ya think it was used for?"

"Whatta ya mean?"

"I mean, it had to've been used for sumpthin'. It just can't"—Janice pauses and glances up at the ceiling—"be sump- thin'."

"Ya think so? Ya don't think it could just be art or some kind'a decoration?"

"No. I think it's a tool of some kind. Besides, if it was art or sumpthin' like that, it would still be used. It would have a purpose."

"Oh, yeah? And what would that be, Miss Fancy Pants?" Dale jabs his fist into his hip, elbow jutting out.

"It would be for lookin' at. For appreciatin'. Maybe these smudges tell a story," Janice says. Her eyes follow her finger as it moves from left to right.

"Yeah?"

"Yeah. Ya know nothin' is made without a purpose."

"Ya sure about that?"

"Sure, I'm sure." Janice pulls back and sits up straight.

"How do ya know?"

"I just do."

"Well, what would ya do if ya didn't?"

"Huh?"

Dale just stares back.

"Ah, forget it." Janice shoos him away with a wave of her hand and turns back to the sunlit pages of her book.

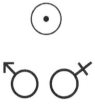

BONES

Dale sweeps some space clear from his work bench with the outside of his left forearm and lays down a small pile of bones that he had cradled in his arms like firewood. Intermittent threads of light slice through the aging boards of the barn's southern wall, illuminating strands of the usually invisible atmosphere of dust around Dale's workspace. Dale recounts the bones, all seven of them, as he spreads them out across the table, grouping ones of a similar shape.

"This could be a rib," he says to himself. "Look how it curves."

Dale sheds his leather gloves to handle the bone with his bare hands. He first glides his forefinger and thumb the length of the supposed rib. Then he turns it over in his hands, holding it at different angles, eyeing it critically. The whole time his forefinger is pressed firmly to one side, his thumb to the other.

"There's three a'these," he says, setting the rib alongside the other two. "And two a'these, I'm assumin' leg bones."

Dale picks one up, surveying its cylindrical nature with the fingers of his right hand.

"That must be part of a shoulder or hip," he says, pointing at a flat bicycle seat shape. "And I'm not sure what that is." The last bone appears to be no larger than Dale's pinky.

Dale shuffles the bones around in several assemblies before settling on one. Taking a step back, he surveys the missing sections and the remaining space available on the work bench, drawing lines in the air with his right forefinger.

"This is a pronghorn."

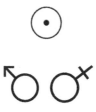

CURSES

Janice dog-ears a page in *Jane Eyre* and closes it as she sighs. She turns off her bedside lamp and sees that Dale's is still on.

"Dale, ya ready ta go ta sleep?" Janice whispers, noticing that Dale is propped up on pillows, looking straight ahead. "Dale," she says more sternly this time.

"Almost," Dale answers faintly, but still with a tinge of gravel in his voice.

"You alright?"

"Yeah, I'm just thinkin'."

"Uh-oh," Janice says as she squirms further under the covers and rests her head on her pillow. "We're all in trouble when that starts happenin'." A moment goes by without a response; Janice turns to look at Dale. He's backlit by the lamp, so only his outline is clearly visible.

"We're supposedly cursed, right?" Dale finally spouts out.

"Huh?" Janice's brows scrunch up.

"Cursed." Dale looks at Janice. "In the Bible, it says we're cursed."

"Since when have you been readin' the Bible?"

"I haven't. That's why I'm askin'.

"Well, yeah." Janice's expression softens. "After Adam and Eve got kicked outta the Garden of Eden, they were punished by God."

"And how were they punished?"

"Men have to spend their days toiling the earth, and women have to suffer the pains of childbirth."

"That's what I thought," Dale says, pointing at her last words.

"So?"

Dale pauses for a moment before asking, "Would ya consider this curse part'a what it means ta be a human?"

"What do ya mean?" Janice asks, rising from her reclined position.

"I mean, do ya think a man is not a man if he doesn't work his land and a woman is not a woman if she don't go through the pain of childbirth?"

Janice swallows hard as she turns her gaze toward the window. "I don't know, Dale. I hadn't thought about it like that."

"I was just thinkin'—if everybody's cursed, but somehow you and me weren't cursed—Well, I guess I was tryin' ta figure out what that would mean. Or why that would be."

"Why do ya say we're not cursed?"

Dale looks down at his hands and starts tracing the pattern on the comforter with his left forefinger. "Because yur not able ta have kids," Dale takes a glance at her reaction, "and I like 'toiling the earth,' as they say. It don't feel like a punishment," he says as his eyes return to his finger.

"Do ya think I like not bein' able ta have children a'my own?"

"Of course not."

"And don't ya think that sounds like a pretty bad curse?"

"Yes, of course. But—"

"But what!?"

"But technically, it's not *the* curse."

"You can technically go fuck yurself, Dale." Janice turns her back to him, lies completely prone, and thrusts the comforter up under her ear.

"I'm sorry. I didn't wanna compare or bring up negative thoughts. I've just been thinkin' 'bout this a lot lately. The point I was tryin'—"

"Yeah, what was yur point?" Janice snarls.

"I guess it's more like the idea I get stuck on is: if God wanted ta curse all people, and we're not cursed—at least not cursed in the same way as other people—then what could God be tryin' ta tell us? I guess it comes down ta not knowing whether this is all a good thang or a bad thang."

Janice blinks a few times, then asks, "Since when do ya believe in God?"

"I never said I believed in God. But if He's even a possibility, then I guess that's enough reason ta fear Him.

"I think it's natural ta fear things we don't understand," Janice says, turning to face the ceiling.

"I don't know if how I'm feelin' is natural," Dale answers, then stares at the palms of his hands.

STARS

The flames of the small fire lap at the desert breeze as Dale supplies it with remnants of sage and shards of dying juniper. "Firewood's hard ta come by out here. Hopefully, this does the trick."

In every direction, Dale's vision is stifled to 20 feet of flickering brush. Beyond that, a black drape envelops him, obscuring his vision from all nightly activities along the horizontal plane. A car hums along the highway in the distance. Dale unrolls the sleeves of his flannel shirt and lies back on the woolen blanket. The clear sky is sprinkled pinhole beams of more-than-million-year-old light.

"Ahh. Now that's a sight I never get sick of. I hear city folk can't see ya so well. That's a shame. But that's gotta mean sumpthin', right?" Dale interlocks his hands and cradles his head, crossing one boot over the other. "Can't see ya all the time, but least we know yur there. That's more than I can say for some. Supposin' it was daylight all the time, though; what'd we think then?" Dale says, scratching his head. Then, extending his right thumb at arm's length and closing his right eye, he starts covering and uncovering patches of stars, making them disappear then reappear. "I can't make ya, but I sure can erase ya," Dale says, chuckling himself into a sigh. "I don't feel no different yet." Turning his gaze toward Moon Reservoir regaining its taut, reflective nature, he asks, "What am I goin' ta do without ya, Janice?"

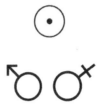

DISCIPLE

Dale plucks the thin wire of a marking flag from the ground and tosses it to the side, the fluorescent pink plastic fluttering until impact. He places the nose of the shovel at the previously marked spot, braces the handle with both hands, and slams his left boot down on the blade's step. With a little prying motion and a second thrust of the foot, the excess dirt is pitched to the right, and the post hole is started. High wispy strands of cotton make poor attempts to diffuse the sun. Dale occasionally pulls at the clinging sleeve or back of his shirt to detach it from his skin.

After several shovelfuls, Dale hears the scraping of earth off his left shoulder. He turns to see Amelia some 20 feet away, pawing the ground repeatedly with her right hoof. The rest of her posture is docile and passive: head up, back straight, tail down. But she's looking straight at Dale, and she won't stop raking the dirt.

"What's wrong, girl? Whatchya doin'?" Dale turns back, sets the shovel blade in the middle of the hole, and jumps with both boots slamming hard on the steps. He lifts out a heaping pile of dirt. Amelia's hoof continues to scrape the earth. "Why don'tchya go be with the others?" he asks as he turns to her again. "That's right. Yur like me. Ya don't mind bein' by yurself." Amelia just stares at Dale and paws the ground. "Alright, let's see whatchya got there."

Dale wriggles through the old fence's tensile wire and walks over to her, shovel in tow. Amelia doesn't flinch. "Yur a persistent cuss. Whatta ya want?" he asks, now standing before her. Amelia keeps pawing the ground. "Ya want me ta dig right there or sumpthin'? Okay, move on back," Dale says, gesturing with the shovel. Amelia shifts her weight and shuffles back a few steps, resetting all four legs firmly on the ground. "I'll humor ya a bit." He shakes his head. "Can't believe I'm takin' orders from a cow. I already have a wife, Amelia."

Dale repeats the process from moments before: slam, pry, lift; slam, pry, lift; slam, pry, lift.

Amelia watches Dale work.

* * *

Soon enough, he has a hole dug that's roughly two feet by two feet. "Sorry, girl, there's nothin' here. Gotta get back ta work." Dale turns and walks back to the eastern fence line, working his way back through the old wires. He sets down the shovel and picks up the posthole digger.

Before he continues digging, Dale looks over to see Amelia peering down into the new hole, nose at its ridge. He snorts a little laugh, shakes his head, and looks to the southern horizon. "Look whatchyur doin' ta us."

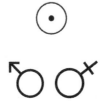

BOREDOM

Dale slices open the end of an 80-pound bag of concrete with the head of his shovel and spreads its contents around the base of a new cedar fence post. He ignores the sound of the pickup and trailer jostling toward him down the dirt road. As the truck slows to a stop, the passenger window rolls down.

"Hey, Dale, if ya work any slower, *yu'll* get stuck in that concrete, not the post," Randall taunts.

"Yeah? And if ya get any fatter, *yu'll* have ta buy a bigger truck," Dale counters.

"Ya gonna put some water in there at least?"

"No," Dale says, tossing the empty concrete bag aside.

"Why not?"

"I've always done it this way. Same's my dad. There's enough moisture in the ground. It sets up just fine."

"Even in this ground?" Randall asks, his eyebrow raised.

"Yeah, I can dig one up if ya wanna see."

"Nah, that's okay. I believe ya. Where do ya want me to put this guy?" Randall says, jabbing his thumb toward the bull in the trailer behind him.

"Just back him in towards the gate there," Dale says, pointing to the northern side of the enclosure. "I'll be right over."

"Alright."

* * *

"So, this here's Rocky," Randall says, swinging open the trailer door. The robust, black bull ambles out from the shade and into the bright light.

"Man, he's sure a good-lookin' animal," Dale says from the other side of the threshold.

"He sure is. Now ya sure ya want to mix this here Angus with all yur Herefords?" Randall asks, stepping toward Dale while keeping his eyes on Rocky.

"Yeah, I'm sure," Dale says, mirroring Randall.

"Ya ain't done that in a long while, haven't ya?"

"I've never done it."

"So why now?"

"Well, I know most ranchers are doin' it these days—the benefits are obvious—"

"Shit, most people would be out here diggin' those post holes with a Bobcat and an auger attachment instead of by hand, ya crazy bastard." Randall removes his cap and wipes his brow with the same forearm. "*You* don't seem to be the kind of guy who does stuff because others are doin' it."

"Ya got me there," Dale says, working his thumb into his calloused palm. "I guess I just got kinda tired a'seein' the same cows each and every year. I know they're different 'n all, but if they always look the same, it makes ya feel like yur not really creatin' new cows; yur just copyin' 'em."

"Hm," Randall half grunts as he looks at Dale, his right eye squinting because of the sun.

"I guess that's just a funny way of sayin' I got bored."

"That's alright, Dale. I'm not tellin' ya how ta run yur

19

ranch. Just a little curious, that's all."

"It's no problem. It's a good question, ac'shally."

"Well, I should probably let Rocky be alone with his new girlfriends," Randall says, pivoting back toward the trailer door.

"Yeah, Rocky, ya ready? There's plenty a tail out there ta chase," Dale calls out. The bull stares out at the herd that is keeping its distance.

Randall swings the trailer door shut. Dale helps him latch it. "So, I'll leave him here a couple weeks?" Randall asks. "And the rate's the same as it has been in the past?"

"Yep. Sixty bucks a week, and ya get first pick'a the offspring."

"Well, it's a pleasure doin' business with ya, Dale," Randall says, hoisting up his pants with both hands before extending his right one for a handshake.

"Same to you," Dale says, reciprocating the gesture.

"Well, I better get back to the homestead. Good luck with yur boredom," Randall says as he waddles his way back to the driver's side of his truck. "I'll see ya in a few weeks."

Randall pulls forward and out onto the dirt road. Dale closes the northern gate and then steps up on the bottom rung, staring out over the pasture to the south. His eyes drift up to some clouds crawling from west to east at the edge of his vision. "I bet ya get bored too, don'tchya?"

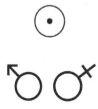

MOTHERHOOD

"Woah, girl," Dale says. He swiftly latches the gate of the side pen as soon as Amelia crosses the threshold. Amelia rears around quickly, her tail up and to the side. "I know ya wanna socialize, but I gotta keep ya 'way from Rocky." Amelia bellows out a long, low-register retort. "I don't wantchya gettin' pregnant," Dale says as he softens his voice, palms stretched wide. Amelia stamps at the base of the gate, kicking up loose dirt, and snorts as she bobs her head up and down. "I know, I know, I know. I'll make it up ta ya. It's just—not part'a the plan." Dale pivots within his shadow under the high, full sun, lowering the brim of his hat, and walks away. Amelia bellows after him repeatedly, each one breaking into a Red Poll falsetto.

* * *

Dale mounts the porch steps with muted boots and shortened strides. The cadence of Janice chopping vegetables travels through the open windows. Dale grabs the screen door handle, pauses, and cocks his head to the south. Amelia's consistent cries permeate the pasture and waft around the house and into Dale's ears. He opens the door and steps inside.

"Don't forget to wipe yur feet," Janice says.

"Huh?"

"Wipe yur feet."

"Whatta ya think I'm doin'?" Dale slides his boots across the welcome mat.

"Just makin' sure," Janice says with a quick glance.

"I don't do it one time, and ya have ta—Ah, shit, never mind." Dale swats the air. "I was gonna try ta tell ya sumpthin', or ask ya sumpthin', rather."

"What's the matter?"

"Nothin', it's just—Can ya hear that?" Dale jabs a thumb over his shoulder.

"What?" Janice stops chopping zucchini into half-moons.

"Listen. Ya hear that?"

"Yeah, who is that?"

"Amelia." Dale sets his hat on the wall hook.

"That ol' girl? Is she hurt? What did ya do ta her?" Janice turns toward Dale, knife still in hand.

"No. I locked her up, so she won't get pregnant."

"Poor thang. Why don't ya let her have some fun?"

"Not Amelia." Dale shakes his head.

"Why not?"

Dale squints his eyes at his living room wall, the southern horizon somewhere on the other side of it.

"Huh, Dale? Why not?" Janice's voice hardens.

Dale's eyes snap back to Janice. "Cuz I don't wanner to," he says as he saunters over to a pitcher of sun tea on the kitchen counter opposite his wife.

Janice snorts. "That's some answer." She turns back to the cutting board, grabs a zucchini, and runs the blade down the length of it. "She knows she's different, ya know. I see her off by herself all the time. Cows are social animals. She should be with the others."

"She's strong." Dale takes a large gulp of tea. "Red Polls don't mind bein' alone."

"She's an outcast, Dale. And Red Polls only got that way because men bred them that way. It's not natural. Besides, it doesn't sound like she wants ta be alone right now." Janice points the knife over her shoulder in the direction of Amelia's cries.

* * *

Janice sits up in bed, her fingers thrum the cover of *An Old-Fashioned Girl* in the lamplight, casting long, shadow spiders across the top blanket. Dale's lamp is off. He lies on his right side, back to Janice. Amelia's bellows are drowning out all other night songs.

"How are *you* asleep?"

"I'm not," Dale answers, voice muffled by his pillows.

"Can ya hear that?"

"A'course I can."

"Well, can't ya do sumpthin' 'bout it?"

"Like what?"

"I don't know, but sumpthin'." Janice pauses, fingers still little horses galloping. "How long's that bull stayin' here?"

Dale slowly rolls to his back. "Rocky's gonna be here a couple weeks. Like usual."

"Suppose she's gonna keep this up the whole time?"

"Can't imagine she can," Dale answers.

"She's never done this before, has she?"

"Nope. First time."

"And ya locker up each time?"

"Yep."

"Gosh! That sound! It reminds me, uh—" Janice trails off.

"Yeah."

"Ya know what I'm thinkin'?"

"Yeah. It's the same sound the mothers would make when we'd take the calves," Dale says softly.

"Yes, that was awful. The way they cried," Janice says, shaking her head, curling her lips and brow into a grimace.

"We don't do it that way no more."

"Thank God. But poor Amelia? What do we do?"

"Try ta sleep."

"Ugh, I can't." Janice thrusts herself free of sheets, blankets, and books and storms out of the room, only pausing to slide into slippers and to grab her cotton robe from the back of a chair.

"Where *you* goin'?" Dale asks as his eyes follow her to the doorway. He blinks a few times, then hears the screen door slap shut.

* * *

Janice carefully crawls back into bed and turns off her lamp. As she pulls the sheets back up toward her chin, her book falls to the floor. She reaches down to pick it up, and, for the first time, Dale can hear the crickets chirping.

"Where'd ya go?" Dale whispers up into the darkness.

"I went to check on Amelia," Janice answers.

"Ya didn't let her out, did ya?" Dale's voice rises in agitation.

"No, I talked ta her."

"Well, how'd ya getter ta quiet down?" Dale's voice calms back down toward a whisper.

"Like I said. I talked ta her."

"Well, whatchya say?"

Janice shakes her head. "Ya wouldn't understand."

"Alright," Dale lets out as a sigh and turns on his right shoulder, away from Janice.

Janice stares up for a few moments before turning toward Dale. "She wants ta be a mother."

"Don't we all."

"Yeah," Janice says, draping her arm over Dale and scooting close. Dale takes her hand and presses it into his chest.

ANGELS

Dale walks along Highway 20 with his left thumb extended, a rolled-up wool blanket under his right arm. The mid-morning sun casts a long shadow warped by the steep camber of the shoulder, marching to the cadence of boots crunching gravel.

He turns his head at the sound of a slowing vehicle behind him, cautiously stepping down the embankment at the sight of the mid-'80s Wagoneer. The passenger side window buzzes down, revealing a woman behind the wheel, the sleeves of a faded Adrian High School sweatshirt pushed up to her elbows.

"Ya need a ride?"

"Yeah, if yur headin' this way," Dale says, gesturing to the west.

"I am. Get in."

Dale opens the passenger door and climbs in. "Thanks, I owe ya one."

"Yeah, ya do. My name's Sheila," she says, extending her hand.

"Dale," he says, shaking it.

"So whatchya doin' out here? It doesn't look like ya got much with ya."

"My car broke down at Moon Reservoir. Started walkin' this mornin'."

"No phone?" Sheila asks, checking her mirrors before accelerating.

"Nope."

"Ah, geez, that doesn't sound like fun. How far of a walk was that?"

"Oh, I'm not sure. What time is it, anyway?"

"Nearly nine-thirty," Sheila says with a quick glance at her small silver watch.

"Yeah, I'm bettin' it was ten miles or so. I think it's fifteen by car, but I walked straight north as the crow flies." Dale draws a straight line in the air with his finger.

"Wow. Ya need anthin' ta drink? I got this bottle a'water right here. Sorry, that's all."

"Nah, I'm alright."

"Ya sure?"

"Yeah."

Dale fixes his gaze out the passenger's side window as Sheila steals frequent glances at him, hands maintaining ten and two.

"Wanna know why I picked ya up?" Sheila asks abruptly.

"Sure," Dale musters.

"Every time I drive through here, I'm in awe of how desolate it is. Ya can go miles without seein' another soul."

"Try livin' out here."

"No thanks. It's much more comfortin' ta know I can just drive through it. Anyhow, it reminds me a'this time I swear I's picked up by angels."

"What?" Dale finally turns from the window to look at Sheila.

"Yeah, when I was a teenager, I got caught walkin' home in a downpour. I was a leavin' a Bible study, and I couldn't call anybody because, ya see, this was before cell phones, *way* before." Sheila nods at Dale with a smile. "And sure enough, 'bout a mile or so into it, a couple pulls up in a white car. They ask me, 'you need a ride?' And I knew no teenage girl should take a ride from strangers, but standin' there, in that instant, all I could think about was how cold I was, my wet clothes clinging to my body; so, I said, 'yes,' and I got in, and they took me home."

"So why do ya think they were angels?" Dale asks with scrunched brows.

"Oh, well, a couple things. One," Sheila keeps count on her fingers, "when I told them where I lived, they said it was on their way, but I swear the car had to do a U-turn when they offered me a ride. So, ya see, they either lied ta me ta be my savior, or I remembered it wrong."

"Lyin' angels makes for a more interestin' story."

"Maybe. But the other fishy thing about it was"—Sheila holds up a second finger—"when I told them where I went ta church, they said they went there too, even though I'd never seen them or their car there before."

"Hm. That's it?"

"Whatta ya mean?"

"Those two things are why ya think they were angels?" Dale asks, one eyebrow arched.

"Well, no." Sheila shakes her head. "But the last one's the hardest to explain. Ya kinda had to be there, ya know?"

"Go on."

"Well, it was just a simple feelin'."

"What was?"

"Well, in that moment that they were backin' outta my driveway, just before my mom started callin' me a tramp for hoppin' in a stranger's car and how my wet clothes weren't leavin' much to the imagination, I felt this strange sense of understandin' come to me like a veil had been lifted, like I had experienced somethin' special. And in that moment, I knew, or at least the fourteen-year-old version of me did," Sheila says with a shrug.

Dale's vision racks focus to the southern horizon. "Ya say it came ta ya?"

"Sorry, what?" Sheila squints at Dale.

"The special feelin'. It came ta ya?"

"Oh, yeah!" Sheila nods in slow succession. "And it had a hard time leavin' too."

"Whatta ya mean?" Dale asks, squinting back at Sheila.

"Well, I'm not sure I believe all that stuff 'bout angels anymore, seein' as how I've never had another experience like it, but I sure remember that feelin'. It had me convinced for the longest time."

"Yeah, I bet," Dale says as he looks at his hands.

"So, anyway, when I saw ya walkin' on the side'a the road this mornin' in the most lonesome stretch of highway in the U.S."—Sheila's hand glides across the view in front of them—"I thought of a fourteen-year-old soaking wet girl clutching her Bible, and I figgered I'd help."

"Are ya an angel?" Dale asks.

"Ha! If only."

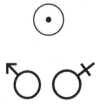

PUHA

Dale steps into Oards Gallery outside of Burns to find himself instantly transported to a world of turquoise, coral, and magenta against the tan of hides. Feet planted, he surveys the entire room, giving every shelf and display case a hard glance. There is too much to take in at once. Not a bare spot exists. Only an endless arrangement of jewelry, paintings, vases, dreamcatchers, moccasins, and so on.

Dale shifts an object wrapped in tissue paper back and forth in his hands as he begins to gingerly step about the room.

When a heron of a woman appears with dangly, beaded earrings, Dale is giving an ornate cradleboard an inspection.

"Well, hello! How are you doing today?" she says, walking toward Dale. "You see anything you like?"

"I just couldn't figger out what this thang was," Dale says, pointing above his head.

"That's a cradleboard." She tilts her head back to peer through the glasses at the end of her nose; her earrings swing back and forth. "It was made by a local Paiute—"

"A what?"

"A cradleboard. They're for carrying newborns around for the first few months or so."

"Oh, I see."

"Do you have children?"

"Nope, the missus couldn't have 'em," Dale says bluntly.

"Oh, I'm sorry to hear that." She crosses her hands over her chest. "I didn't mean—"

"Who'd ya say made this?"

"A local Paiute artist. That's where we get many of the things you see around you."

"Right here from the reservation?"

"Yes, indeed."

"Huh, who woulda thunk?"

"Yes, we're very blessed to have so many talented artists living so close to us. Do you live here in Burns?" she says, pointing back down the highway.

"No," Dale says, shaking his head. "I live out west a'ways. In between Riley and Hampton."

"So, what brings you out here today?"

"Well, I was hopin' for some help, ac'shally."

"Alright, what kind?"

"I found this on my property." Dale unwraps the turnip-shaped object from the tissue paper. "And I can't tell what it is. I had a feelin' it was Indian, so I came in here hopin' I'd get some answers."

"Ooh, yeah. It looks like you came to the right place," she says, squinting through her narrow lenses.

"Ya can tell what it is?"

"Yeah, it looks like you have yourself a Paiute seed jar."

"Ya sure? Ya can tell that quickly?"

"Pretty sure. You mind if I take a closer look?" she asks, extending a flat palm.

"Sure." Dale slowly hands over the seed jar.

"You can see that it's made of twine, which is real common

31

for Paiute seed jars. It's worn down so much it's kind of lost its texture." She rotates the seed jar with the tips of her fingers. "In some places, it just looks like it's caked with dirt. But I'm sure it's Paiute."

"Yur not Indian, are ya? I mean, I'm not tryin' to be rude or nothin', but how can *you* be sure if yur not Indian?"

She purses her lips for a moment, releases them, and then calmly responds, "What is that over there?"

"What? Where?"

"That thing over there made of—" She holds her arm up, pointing just as Dale did. "It looks like wood, or some hide, and some willow maybe, oh, and beads. You were looking at it earlier."

"The cradleboard?"

"Yeah, that's it. Now how did you know that, considering you're not Indian and all?"

"Ya told me."

"That's right, and do you think you could spot another one if you saw it some other place?"

"Okay, okay. I see what you're doin'. Ya made yur point."

"Good. I'm glad. Now what you have here, sir, is a Paiute seed jar," she says, handing it back to Dale. "Are you wanting to sell it? If so, I'm sure I could put you in contact with someone who would be interested."

"Nah, this ain't for sellin'. I just wanted ta know what it was or what it was used for," Dale says as he envelops the seed jar in tissue paper once again.

"You're holding a fairly rare artifact there. May I ask you what you plan on doing with it?"

"I don't know yet. I think that learnin' what somethin's made for changes yur—yur outlook on it. I'll think on it. Maybe I'll keep it; maybe I'll give it to a museum. Who knows?"

"Well, is there anything else I can help you with?" she asks with folded hands and a thin smile. They begin walking toward the exit.

"I guess I have one more question."

"Alright, go ahead." Her long earrings sway as she nods.

"Did the first Indian ta make one'a these do it because he needed somethin' ta collect his seeds in, or did he make it and then realize it was good for collectin' seeds?" Dale asks.

"Now that I can't answer with certainty, and I don't think anyone without a time machine could, but I believe it was created with the purpose of storing seeds. That seems to the be the pattern of development for Native American cultures— and all people for that matter," she says.

"That's exactly right." They stop in front of the glass door.

"May I ask why that matters to you? It doesn't change what you're holding in your hand."

"It changes everything," Dale says seriously, looking down at the seed jar.

"Excuse me?"

"I'm sorry," Dale says, snapping his attention back. "I find these sorts'a thangs interestin'. I guess I spend too much time outside workin' by muhself." Dale scratches his head. "It's probly all the dust that's been blown in my ears. I'm not sure."

"You know, that could be a good thing, connecting to nature. The Paiute thought power could live in things like the sun and the moon and the wind." Dale's eyes widen as she speaks. "Yeah, if you were a Paiute man, you might wake up every day and pray to the sun to bless your hunt."

"Like for a pronghorn, maybe?"

"Yes, exactly." Her eyebrows rise. "But only shamans could harness that power themselves."

"So how do ya become one'a them shamans?"

"Well, you can't really try to become one."

"No?"

"No. Being a shaman was traditionally not something you sought. It had to come to you. Like a blessing. You were either born with it, or the spirits bestowed it upon you later in life."

"So, you sorta had to be chosen?"

"Yes."

"And how would they choose ya?"

"They'd usually receive a special dream."

"So ya had ta be asleep?"

"Well, that's usually how dreams work," she says with a smile. "But sadly, shamans hardly exist anymore." She looks out beyond the highway. Dale stares straight at her. "They were healers, you know. So, most have essentially been replaced by western medicine."

"Most, ya say?" Dale tightens his grip on the seed jar.

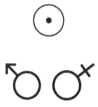

LIVING

"What'll ya have, Dale?" a voice rasps out from behind a full beard.

"Whatever's cold," Dale says as he takes a seat at the bar.

"Be more specific."

"Coors."

"Coors Light okay?"

"Yeah, that's fine."

"Unless ya wanna bottle. I've got Coors in a bottle."

"Nah, that's alright." Dale scans the mounted heads of pronghorns and mule deer while Rick, the bartender, fills a mug.

"So, what brings ya inta town on this fine Saturday?" A bit of head sloshes over the side as Rick sets down the beer.

"Just the weekly supply run," Dale says as he grabs the handle.

"Anythang in particular?"

"Nope. Not really."

"Well, let me know if ya need anythang else," Rick says,

then slides down the bar to help someone else.

"Alright."

Dale turns on his stool to face Central Pastime's only big-screen TV. The A's and the Braves are playing an afternoon game.

As Dale tilts his mug back, a man from a table barks out, "Hey, Dale! Is that you?" Dale turns toward the voice. "It's me, Jerry." His arm is stretched high over his head.

"Hey, Jerry, how's it goin'?" Dale asks, lifting his mug in recognition.

"Good. And how 'bout yurself?"

"Nothin' ta complain about."

"Oh, shit. There's always sumpthin' ta complain about. Come over here and join us." Jerry waves with his whole arm.

"Nah, I'm okay."

"Nonsense. Come on over."

"Ya sure?"

"Yeah, pull up a chair. Ya guys scoot over and make room." Jerry shoos the other guys with the backs of his hands. "Dale, this is Hugh McGowan, Craig Hines, and Bill Grant. Fellas, this is Dale Samuel," Jerry says, pointing around the circle.

"Hi."

"How's it goin'?"

"Howdy."

"Nice ta meet ya guys," Dale responds, then leans back in his chair.

"So, Dale, ya still workin' that piece a'land ya got out there?" Jerry asks, foam clinging to his mustache.

"Yup."

"See guys, Dale here lives an hour or so toward Bend—is that about right, Dale?"

"Yeah, give or take a few minutes."

"Truly out in the middle of nowhere." Jerry sweeps his hands wide, almost knocking over a beer. "Oops."

"Whatta ya do out there? Ya in cattle?" Bill asks.

"Yeah, I try ta be." Dale's eyes follow the question.

"That's how I know Dale. Bought a few cows off'a him over the years," Jerry interjects.

"How much land ya got?" Craig asks.

"'Bout thirdy acres."

"That's a lotta work for one man," Jerry says.

"I guess."

"Ya ever think about doin' sumpthin' else?" Jerry continues. "We're not gettin' any younger."

"Like what?"

"Well, Hugh's a mechanic. Craig and I are with the Public Works Department, checkin' water lines. And Bill works at the golf course. Don't worry," Jerry says, shaking his palm in front of Dale. "He's not one'a them arrogant bastards. Point is, regular guys like us don't need ta work so hard anymore. We're cursed, but we're not that cursed."

Dale leans forward in his seat. "Suppose I don't feel cursed."

"Well then, shit, more power to ya! I'm just sayin' there's easier ways ta make a livin'. That's all."

"That's the difference right there." Dale points a calloused finger.

"What?"

"While you guys are makin' a livin', I'm just livin'.'"

"Whatta ya mean?" Bill asks.

"I mean, there's nothin' I do durin' a day's work that's not directly related ta keepin' me and my wife alive." Dale sneaks a quick glance at the pronghorn hanging on the wall. "I've thought about it quite a bit over the years. I just can't stand the thought a'doin' somethin' all day ta earn enough money ta stay alive. I'd just rather cut ta the chase, ya know? No offense," Dale says, leaning back again.

"None taken," Craig says.

"Shit, Dale. I haven't heard ya talk this much in my whole goddamn life. I didn't know ya were such a philosopher." Jerry bursts into laughter as he slaps Dale on the back. "Maybe ya should get out more." The other three chuckle until their efforts are stifled by beer. Jerry adds more foam to his mustache. "Hey, Rick, another round on me."

* * *

Dale walks out to his truck after a few beers and climbs inside. He opens the glove box and pulls out a turnip-shaped object wrapped in tissue paper. "So yur a seed jar, huh?" He traces its circumference with one finger as he rotates the seed jar in the other hand. "And I bet after all this time, yur still okay with it."

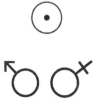

FEELING LONELY

The radio emits static in Dale's Chevy Silverado humming west on Highway 20. In front of him, the road seems endlessly straight, becoming a blur of earth, asphalt, sky, and heat somewhere near the horizon. The sun is not yet in his eyes. With no traffic in view, Dale looks out to his left at the vast and open landscape peppered by sage, a rolling hill or two, and an occasional western juniper standing in bleak isolation.

"It's so lonely out here," Dale says aloud, although without a passenger next to him. "But I like it. Maybe I shouldn't say 'lonely,' that sounds bad." He hesitates, checking the road in front of him with small, sideways glances. "It makes ya definitely feel alone, but like yur alone for a reason."

Dale turns off the static and takes a look out the passenger side window. The topography is all scrunched up on that side, limiting what can be seen, making it all foreground with no depth of field.

Dale glances quickly at the glove box and then returns his

attention to the sprawling south. "And ta think, I bet humans've never touched some'a those places." He pauses for a moment. "But then, what's it there for? What's the point?" Dale finishes this question as the road bends to the right and an oncoming car reveals itself to him. He secures the wheel in both hands and fixes his gaze with a furrowed brow, the sun now creeping into his eyes.

A SINGLE LIFE

Dale stands in the aisle of JC's Best Buys in Burns, eyeing the only two mattresses he can find in the store. His boots sand the plywood flooring as he pivots.

"Can I help ya, sir?" asks a mousy woman approaching with inches of graying roots visible along her part line.

"Yeah, I need a new mattress."

"Well, we don't sell any new ones. Yu'll have to go to John Day or Ontario or, um, Bend for that."

"What are these, then?" Dale asks, pointing.

"Gently used ones," she says, coming to a stop next to Dale's left elbow.

"Are these all ya got?"

"Yes, sir. A queen and a full." She gently folds her hands at her waist.

"I'll take the full."

"You got grandkids growin' up or family comin' inta town?"

"Nah, I just—" Dale shuffles his feet. "I just don't need that big a bed no more."

"Ah, I see. Ya got a truck out front?" She quickly turns and gestures to the back of the store. "I can have one of the boys bring it out ta ya."

"Nah, I got it," Dale says, grabbing the long edges of the mattress.

"Ya sure?"

"Yeah." Dale turns it on its side and readjusts his grip.

"Okay then, follow me," she says with a wave of her hand. Dale hoists the mattress with a grunt and complies. "Yeah, sleepin' in a big bed all by yurself can get awful lonesome." She pauses, but Dale doesn't reply. "After my first husband left me, and we were livin' *way* out in the country then"—she waves both arms toward the horizon—"I moved back inta town real quick." She circles around the register. "Got remarried real quick, too," she adds with a chuckle.

Dale sets the mattress down. "And why do ya think that was?"

"The movin' or the marryin'?"

"Both, I guess."

"I don't know." She works the register. "My mother would say it's because I know my rightful place. That'll be fordy dollars even," she says, interjecting her own chatter. "But I think all that empty space makes me nervous. Like somethin's missin'." Dale hands her the money. "It's kinda why I'm one'a the few that don't mind how this town is growin'. I guess that's what happens when you come from a big family."

"Yeah, I've never had that problem."

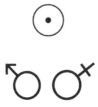

TRICKSTER

Dale lays two new bones down on the workbench alongside his partially assembled skeleton. They both are long, thin bones, but one is nearly twice the length and diameter of the other.

Taking off his gloves, his eyes survey each item on the table. The fingers on his right hand thrum a dull rhythm that echoes off the wooden surface as he bites his lower lip.

"Okay," Dale says, reaching for the larger of the two new bones with his right hand. "Maybe *you* go here." He swaps out a bone he had lying in the area of the upper front leg with his left hand. "And that means this guy must go here." He reaches across his body and sets it where a lower rear leg would be. Dale's eyes then flit back and forth between the fragmented extremities and the smaller of the two new bones. "This one looks pretty similar ta these. But I've already got four'a them." Dale picks up the smaller bone, then sets it back down. "Hm." He shifts his weight, and bits of straw crackle under his boots. "Or, if I slide this one up so, then this might go here," Dale says, repositioning the bone he already moved, and slots the new one in its place. "Or maybe—" Dale puts his hands on his hips. "Sheesh, yur one tricky pronghorn."

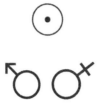

LULLABY

The pitchfork tines displace the dirt around them. Dale's hands drape over the end of the handle in crisscross fashion. His chin rests comfortably on the backs of his gloved hands as he watches Janice kneeling down in her garden studying one of her tomato plants. She hums a soft melody that diffuses quickly in the wind. Dale leans into it, using the pitchfork to balance, hands shifting slightly, causing stubble to flex and bend against leather.

"Whatchya singin'?"

"Oh, Jesus!" she says, her shoulders jerking up. "Ya startled me."

"Sorry, I's just curious."

"Oh, it's nothin'."

"It didn't sound like nothin'. It was nice. It sounded like a lullaby." Dale lifts his chin up from his gloves. "If I didn't have all this work ta do, I'd lay here and take a nap."

Janice's mouth curves into a slight smile, then she sits back against her heels and rests her hands on her thighs. "It's somethin' my mother used to hum in the mornin's as she was gettin' us ready for school—or at night when she was givin' us a bath."

"How come I've never heard it before?" Dale asks, wrinkles multiplying on his forehead.

"I'm sure ya have. Ya just don't remember."

"What are the words?"

"That's what's funny. There aren't any. At least I never heard my mom sing 'em."

"Hm, can you hum it again?"

"Don't be silly," Janice says, breaking eye contact.

"I'm not—look, don't be embarrassed. Ya figure after twenny-five years a'marriage, ya couldn't get embarrassed anymore. Look, yur blushin' and everythang." Dale points a gloved finger.

"Twenny-six."

"Huh?"

"Twenny-six years a'marriage," Janice says, rolling her eyes.

"Oh, even better yet. They say the twenny-sixth year is when embarrassment stops happenin' anymore. Come on." Dale beckons with the same hand. "Let me hear it again."

"No." Janice shakes her head. "It's awkward with ya standin' there lookin' down on me."

"I was standin' here watchin' ya a second ago, and ya were singin' like a bird."

"Because I didn't know ya were there. I thought I was alone."

"Pretend yur alone now. Pretend I'm not standin' here."

"I can't."

"Sure ya can. Some people spend their whole lives pretendin' they *know* sumpthin's there—" Dale says, looking up to the sky. "Ya just have ta pretend ya don't know I'm here for a few seconds." Dale looks back down at Janice.

Janice's eyes move from Dale's to the side of the house,

seemingly unfocused. She hums one note and cuts herself off immediately. "It's hard," she says through a sideways glance. "Once ya know someone's there, it's tough to pretend they're not."

"Ain't that the truth?" Dale's head swivels slightly toward the southern horizon and back again. "Try one more time. I'll even close my eyes. That way, no one will be watchin' ya."

"Alright. But then ya have to stop buggin' me and let me get back ta what I was doin'."

"Okay."

"Now close yur eyes."

"Alright, they're closed."

Janice begins to softly hum the same tune as before. Dale turns his ear to the sound, the sun warm on his face, the wind gently tugging at the brim of his hat. "Hm hm hm-hm-hm hmm hm. Hm hm-hm-hm-hm hmm hmm. Hm hm hm-hm-hm hmm hm. Hm hm-hm-hm-hm hmm hmm—" Janice lets the last note fade into silence. Dale opens his eyes and sees Janice tending to the plants once more.

"Thank ya. That was nice."

"Yur welcome."

"Can I bug ya for one more thang?"

"What?" Janice pauses.

"Can ya drive the truck? I need ta feed the cows."

"Yeah, I'll be there in a minute," she says without looking.

"Alright," Dale says and begins to walk away. After several strides, the faint sound of humming can be heard, but he doesn't turn around. He only smiles.

* * *

"I'm ready," Dale hollers over his right shoulder as he pats the left rear fender of his truck. Janice puts the truck in drive and eases it forward along the uneven terrain, inching as close as she can to the western edge of the pasture. Dale steadies himself with a wide stance in front of a heap of dry alfalfa as the truck rumbles forward, pitchfork balanced across his left thigh, gloved hands wrapped tight around the top and bottom of the handle. The cows notice the truck and amble toward the fence line. Dale thrusts the pitchfork into the alfalfa and heaves it over the fence.

"Is that alright?" Janice calls back.

"Yeah," Dale grunts out.

As he falls into a rhythm, a disheveled olive-green stripe emerges down the length of the pasture, interrupted by soft brown and white heads bobbing up and down. Dale hums Janice's lullaby as he works, but it's carried away by the breeze before it reaches the cab of the truck.

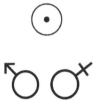

HEAT

Quail scamper in front of Dale as he marches to the center of his pasture to check on Rocky's progress. "How come ya don't just move ta the side, ya little pea-brains?" The sun is high and relentless, the air still. The sky is a spotless blue blanket pulled taut.

Rocky sniffs the back of a heifer who's attentively standing amongst a group of resting herdmates. "There ya go, Rocky. She looks nice and ready." Rocky takes notice of Dale and looks directly at him, shaking a fly off his ear. "Go on, whatta ya waitin' for? This is what yur here ta do." Dale takes a glance to the south at the sound of his own words and then back to Rocky, who's again sniffing the heifer's rear end. "I can see she's all slicked up with mucus. Can't you? She's more than ready." At that moment, she backs her glistening posterior into Rocky's nose, causing the bull to violently shake his head in agitation, startling the young female. Rocky once again cranes his neck to observe Dale. "I'm payin' good money for ya, Rocky. Do yur job," Dale says through clenched teeth.

Stepping forward, he implores the bull with flailing arms. Rocky rears his head and snorts in response to Dale's advance, then he turns around, facing opposite the heifer, tucks his front legs underneath him, and eases down to the ground, staring off to the west. "Damn you, Rocky!" Dale squats down, fingers picking at the dirt in front of him. "Maybe I *am* cursed." Dale blindly chucks a clod over his left shoulder. A covey of quail pip, flutter, and scatter.

Moments later, they return to where they were before.

DRAGON COUGH

Dale watches a small fire grow at the center of a shallow pit halfway between the patio and alfalfa field. The sun is a golden stone sinking behind the western horizon. An ocean of rolling clouds paints the ceiling of the sky, cooling from tangerine to coral as they ripple from their catalyst.

He sets a can of gas down just outside the small, freshly created berm surrounding the pit. "I guess now's the time."

Dale turns to retrieve the queen-size mattress leaning up against the back of the house. He grips it by the long edge and hoists it off the ground the six inches necessary to shuffle his way to the fire. With a hurling motion, propelled by a short grunt, Dale tosses the mattress directly on top, smothering much of the blackened scrap-wood teepee.

He quickly snatches the gas can at his feet and begins to generously pour, straight-armed, onto the center of the mattress, trying to stand clear of the splatter he hears and feels more than sees.

Soon, the stifled flames trying to wrestle their way free

from underneath and liquid trickling from the central puddle connect, and suddenly an orange tendril races to the middle and explodes in one big dragon cough. Dale reflexively steps back, almost stumbling, and corkscrews away from the burst, shielding his face with his free arm. "Whoa! That oughtta do it."

Dale retreats to the patio to exchange the gas can for a crumpled-up bundle of sheets; they smell of day-old human feces. He carries them to what is now a pillar of flame licking at the fluorescent clouds fading to plumes of smoky sapphire and tosses them in. White-hot fingers crawl outward from the center and begin to consume the entirety of the mattress. The smell of gasoline becomes overpowered by the even more incongruous synthetic stench of polyester, foam, and metal being burned.

Dale steps back onto the patio to watch the fire burn as the sun finally disappears. The rusty-gold fountain remains as the only source of light.

He stares at it hard.

* * *

Working in the dull glow of the patio light, Dale shovels the last bit of dirt on top of the smoldering metal skeleton of the mattress. He plunges the shovel's blade into the loose, dusty fill, wipes his brow with the sleeve of his shirt, and turns to the south. "What happens now?"

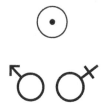

BEING ABLE

Dale swings open the wooden door of A Taste of the Ranch with his left hand; his right removes his hat and simultaneously wipes sweat from his brow with the long sleeve of his thin cotton shirt, now a clinging, wet bandage. Stepping into the soft yellow light of the several solitary fixtures and out of the blaring midday sun brings cool relief to the back of Dale's neck and shoulders. His eyes take a moment to adjust. Janice is waiting on a table of customers in the far corner. Dale finds a seat at the counter.

"What'll ya have?" Lynette, the other waitress, asks, walking a leaning tower of a burger to a man at the end of the counter.

"I'm just here ta ask Rusty sumpthin'."

"No food?"

"I wasn't really—"

"Come on!" she says, waddling toward him. "I know ya can smell that roast beef cookin' back there. Today's special. Comes with potato salad and beans."

"If I eat all that, I won't get any'a my work done this afternoon," Dale says, rubbing his belly with both hands.

"Let's test yur theory."

"I don't know. How 'bout a piece a pie?"

"Pie?" Lynette cocks her head back. "Janice don't bring ya none home?"

"She does." Dale nods. "But she says I take too long ta eat it. By the time I get a hankerin' for it and open the fridge, it's gone. She beats me to it every time."

"A piece a'pie it is then. Cherry cream okay?"

"Sounds great. And can ya tell Rusty I need 'em when he's gotta chance?"

"Sure thang, hun," Lynette says, carrying place settings out to an empty table, rocking on her stumpy legs.

Janice circles back behind the counter to hang a ticket in the kitchen window. "Ya checkin' up on me today or what?" she asks without even stopping to look him in the eye.

"Just came ta ask Rusty 'bout that ol' fridge."

"Lynette getchya taken care of?"

"Yeah."

"Havin' the special?"

"Nah, a piece'a pie."

"Ya must not be workin' hard enough if that's all the appetite ya got." Janice pauses just long enough to plant her feet.

"Pie just sounded good, that's all." Dale shrugs.

"Alright. I gotta help these people. See ya at home?"

"Yeah."

"Oh, here's Rusty," Janice says, pointing with the pen in her hand.

"Hi, Dale. What do I owe the pleasure? Yur not here ta take Janice away from us, are ya?" Rusty says with fists on hips.

"No. She likes workin', and I don't mind."

"Plus, I bet the extra time alone doesn't hurt, eh?" Rusty jokes, a big smile crawling out from under his thick, bristly mustache.

"I don't think extra time alone is sumpthin' I need more of," Dale says frankly, sneaking a glance out the window to the south.

"Yur already batty enough as it is?"

"Yeah, sumpthin' like that. Listen," Dale pauses as Lynette sets down his pie: dark red cherries on a thick pillow of cream. "Janice told me ya was gettin' a fancy new refrigerator."

"I am."

"I was wonderin' if I could buy the old one from ya."

"Depends on what yur offerin'. Besides, what do ya wanna industrial fridge for?"

"I could pay ya some, and the rest I could trade ya beef for. A few sides a'beef turned into burgers and steaks could more than pay for a fridge, couldn't it?"

"That's a decent proposition, but I don't wanna wait 'til the fall ta get paid."

"That's what the fridge's for." Dale takes his first bite of pie. "I wanna be able ta slaughter year-round," he says with his mouth full.

"I see." Randy wipes his hands back and forth across his apron. "Well, why do ya wanna do that?"

"I don't know if it's so much 'I wanna do it,' I just wanna be able ta do it." Dale swallows. "Make sense?"

"Sorta."

"I just don't like not bein' able ta do sumpthin'. Ya know, like limitations." Dale gestures with the bright red prongs of his fork.

"I think I follow ya. Anyway, how much could ya gimme up front?"

"Six hunnerd."

"I suppose that'll do."

"So, it's a deal?"

"Yeah, I think so," Rusty says as they shake hands. "Enjoy yur pie."

"I will. And thank ya."

* * *

Dale eats all but one bite of pie, places a five-dollar bill on the counter, and leaves.

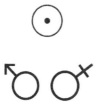

CIRCLES

Dale slices through the alfalfa with the scythe in a wide sweeping motion, keeping the blade parallel to the ground at all times. His boots trail behind, crunching what's left of the dewy stalks, harmonizing with the metronomic rhythm of the scythe. A soft and smooth backstroke to two o'clock, right foot inching forward. An aggressive yet controlled forward stroke to ten o'clock, left foot in sync. A fresh windrow forms in an asymmetrical wake.

Dale finishes a pass and turns around to begin another, heading straight back down to the western edge of the alfalfa field. He looks to his right to see the seven completed windrows. Then to his left to see hundreds of feet of uncut alfalfa. Then back to the right. Back to the left.

Pausing at the edge of the field, Dale looks up over the purple-topped alfalfa to the southern horizon. "And ta think. I'm gonna be back out here in no time." He snaps his eyes back down to the ground, lines up another swath, and begins to cut.

* * *

Dale walks up to the front porch to find Janice knocking the dust out of their mats and rugs with a wooden rug beater, each one strewn over the railing, exhaling a small cloud after every whack. Dale watches her work as she inches her way down the tiny L-shaped assembly line.

"Oh, I didn't see ya there," Janice says, finally noticing Dale, letting the tip of the rug beater rest on the porch.

"No problem. I was just admirin' yur work," Dale says, his left forearm leaning on the porch's corner post, left leg casually draped over the right.

"Oh, this?" Janice asks with a scrunched brow. "There's not much to it, really."

"Still. I can tell ya's got a process. A way ya likes ta do it."

"Yeah. I suppose I got routines for most thangs. But that's normal, isn't it?"

"A'course." Dale nods.

"Where's all this comin' from anyway?"

"I was just thinkin' 'bout sumpthin' as I was workin' the alfalfa"—Dale taps his temple—"then I come over here, and yur workin' reminded me a'the same thang."

"You? Thinkin' again? Whew." Janice exhales and shakes her head, then lifts the rug beater back up and fixes her grip.

"Aren'tchya gonna ask what I was thinkin' 'bout?"

"I guess I don't have much of a choice," Janice says, lowering the rug beater again. "Go on, Dale."

"Well, let me ask ya a question instead," Dale says, straightening himself up. "Do ya think repetition is a good thang or a bad thang?"

"Well, that all depends on what I'm repeatin'."

"A'course. At least that's what I thought too. But I was thinkin' how sometimes I'll do a pretty unenjoyable thang, and if I do it enough times, ya know, once it becomes part'a the routine, as ya said, it starts to become rather tolerable. Sometimes even downright enjoyable."

"So, ya think it's good?" Janice asks, shuffling down the porch toward Dale.

"Well, no. Not exactly. Cuz sometimes it works the opposite." Dale shifts his boots in the soft dirt. "Like, I'll do sumpthin' I like, but if I do it enough times, sometimes that takes all the fun out of it."

"So, maybe repetition makes bad things better and good things worse," Janice says, taking a few more small steps. "Maybe it balances thangs out."

"Yeah, except sometimes ya can repeat the good thangs, and ya never get tired of 'em," Dale says, finally taking a stride toward Janice and craning his neck up. She is right above him on the porch now. "Like that Patsy Cline song yur always listenin' to. Ya never seem ta get tired a'that. What's it called?"

Janice looks up to the eastern skyline and smiles. "'Pick Me Up on Your Way Down.'"

"Yeah, that one. So, whatta ya make a'that?"

"I don't know, Dale. But now yur talkin' in circles."

"Yeah," Dale says, taking a peek to the south. "Maybe that's all it's suppose'ta do."

POINTLESS

Dale peels back the flannel sheets usually reserved for winter-time and climbs into his full-size bed. The burgundy sheets spill out from the seafoam-colored summer top blanket and gather on the floor. Dale lies on his back and runs his hands lightly through his chest hair while staring up at the ceiling. "Sleepin's when I feel most alone," Dale says softly and then arches his neck to look toward the window, which is now directly overhead. "Is this what it's like? Ya know—like all the time?" The cool night air breathes in at one of its regular intervals, rattling the blinds a bit to break up the crickets' song.

Dale looks back toward the ceiling, which is hard to make out because of the cloud-covered moon. "Twenny-six years is a long time," Dale says, letting out a long sigh. His right hand reaches inside his briefs to adjust himself. "All that time with just one woman." Dale begins to fondle himself. "I wonder what Angela Holbrook looks like now."

Dale slides his underwear down to his knees and flops his

penis back and forth as it gets heavier in his hand. "I can still remember the first day of tenth grade." Dale squeezes his eyes shut. He's now stroking his hard penis. "That summer dress— with the buttons too far apart." Dale pumps his hand faster. "Yeah, that's it."

A small gust of wind blows the blinds against the window frame more violently, breaking Dale's concentration. He opens his eyes and pauses his hand. Turning over to get up on his knees, he faces the window, his right hand still gripping his erection. The blinds swing in lazy circles.

Then Dale lets out a sigh. "What's the point? It doesn't lead ta nothin'." Dale lets go of his penis and waits until he goes soft. Then, he wriggles on his underwear, plops on his side, and closes his eyes.

"It's too damn hot for these sheets anyway," Dale says, kicking his feet completely free of the bedding.

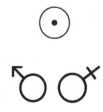

VALIDATION

Dale pulls the plastic palpation sleeve up his left arm until it meets his shoulder. Pumping lubricant from an industrial-sized bottle, he fills his left hand with translucent goo. "Okay, girl, here we go." Dale lifts the tail with his right hand and coats the heifer's rectum with his left as a small shiver dominos up the hairs along her spine. Cupping his hand with his palm up, Dale gently but firmly presses his arm through the rectum, twisting his arm as he does so to minimize its width. "Don't worry. This'll only take a minute." Once directly in between the hips, Dale sweeps along the left side of the cavity with an open hand. From there, he starts searching for the hard, pinky-sized cervix. "There it is. Nice!" As he grabs it, he can tell that it's tipping forward to a noticeable degree. "Now I just have ta check out one more thang." Dale works his fingers down the cervix and locates the uterine horns. Separating them with his fingers, he then traces the length of each one with his forefinger and thumb in a soft pinching manner, searching for fluid. He finds some in each horn. As Dale retracts his arm, a little excess of feces falls out. He shifts his weight quickly, so it doesn't land on his boot. With a pat of the hand on her rump, Dale says, "Finally, one'a ya's is pregnant."

A GOOD LIFE

The crack of the .44 rings in Dale's ears, but the barn's walls can't suffocate the sound completely; the muffled intonation of the gunshot echoes over the sand and sagebrush. All of the cow's 1,200 pounds crumple to the ground with a resounding thud. "Ya were a good girl," he says, looking the cow in the eye. "Don't take it personal."

Dale kneels down on the concrete slab and sinks his six-inch blade in right above the breastbone. Cutting diagonally toward the head, careful to keep the hide from getting into the flesh, his hands work the knife away from him, severing the major veins and arteries. A dam of blood breaks free into a sprawling pool; the smell of iron mixes with that of manure. The legs involuntarily spasm and kick, catching Dale in the ear as he finishes the cut. "Whoa, girl. Easy there," Dale says calmly. "Funny how the body don't know it's dead for a while." Dale wipes the blade and plunges it into the side of the neck, carving its way through a full circumference of flesh. Dale snorts. "I bet we're no different. Heck, with a lot'a people, it's probly the opposite; don't know they're alive."

Dale reaches behind him, trading the knife for the meat saw. "Ya know ya didn't deserve this"—making eye contact again—"but it's just the way it goes." He pauses, then shakes his head. "Easy for me ta say, huh?" Placing his left hand firmly on the jaw, Dale saws the spinal column with his right.

"Ya lived a good life. Ya did what yur supposed ta do. Ya just didn't know it," Dale says, facing the cow's severed head in his outstretched arms. "Well, ya best not watch the rest." Dale sets the head down next to the waste bucket, turning it to face the opposite wall.

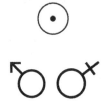

WINDOWS

A steady stream from the faucet rinses off the freshest crimson from Dale's hands. With the bar of soap, he works up an immense lather, then scrapes with milky white fingers at blood already dried a dark brown in his nail beds. Janice shuffles into the kitchen. The running sink is the only sound as the sideways light of dawn fully breaks.

"Ya ever think'a eyes?"

"What? What nonsense are—Can't ya just say *good mornin'*?"

"Mornin'. Sorry, I was just standin' here thinkin'."

"Again?"

"Ya know how the look in someone's eyes is what makes 'em seem—well, seem alive?" Dale continues.

"Yeah, the eyes *are* the windows ta the soul," Janice says as she makes her way to the cupboards.

"Who said that?" Dale asks, snapping his head around.

"Oh, I don't know. It's just a-sayin'."

"Anyway, ya know what I'm talkin' 'bout?" Dale asks,

rinsing the lather off to reveal spots of blood still clinging to his hands.

"Yeah, I think so."

"Well, I was noticin' this mornin' that the eyes are what make someone, at least a cow, look dead too."

"Yeah, and?" Janice sets out a ceramic bowl, some plates, and a whisk.

"I just thought it was strange. Strange ta think a part'a somethin', and a small part too, could be where ya look to see if somethin's alive or ta see if it's dead." Dale begins washing his hands a second time.

"Why's that strange? Seems perfectly natural ta me."

"Ya just say that because that's how it is."

"Huh?" Janice asks, scanning the refrigerator's top shelf.

"Just because somethin's natural doesn't mean it's not strange. Maybe lots'a thangs are strange if ya look close."

"I think the proof a'that is standin' in my kitchen."

"Anyway, what I realized this mornin', the strange part that is, is that the eye itself doesn't look any different. It doesn't change colors, it doesn't dry up, it doesn't grow cloudy. So somehow, somethin' that doesn't really change changes how somethin' looks, changes how alive it looks."

"Ya spend too much time in the sun yesterday?"

"Probly. And every day before that too," Dale says, finally drying his hands gently with a dishtowel.

"Make sure ya rinse off the soap."

"The soap?"

"Yeah, I don't want no blood on it the next time I use it."

"Keepin' soap clean, huh?" Dale mutters softly as he complies. "How ya expect ta keep the soap clean if yur constantly rubbing it on dirty thangs?" Dale addresses Janice again, taking a quick glance at the eastern horizon as he does so. "Seems strange."

"It's called *cleanliness*."

"But is it natural?" he says with a smirk that she turns her back to.

"Ya want some eggs?"

"Yeah, I think I have time."

FEELING NOTHING

Dale hammers a fence staple into a cedar post, bracing the top strand of tensile wire in place. His eyes rack focus from his leather-clad left thumb and forefinger to a silver pickup driving down the dirt road, kicking up a fine-powder rooster tail pulled sideways by a gusty wind. Dale stands up to watch it pass by his house and slow to a stop as it eclipses the southern fence line. The passenger window rolls down as Dale marches toward the Dodge Ram, securing his hat to the top of his head with his left hand.

"Where's Janice?" Rusty says, but it's lost in the wind. Dale cups his ear with his right hand as he sees the driver's lips move. Rusty then jams the truck in park and climbs out of the driver's side and around the front of the idling engine to meet Dale at the edge of the road. Dale lowers his hand from his ear. "I said, 'Where's Janice?' She didn't come in ta work today. I've been callin' all afternoon," Rusty says, squinting into the wind and evening sun from under a red cap.

"She's not here. When I woke up this mornin', her car was gone."

"Yur shittin' me." Dale slowly shakes his head. "Really? What she do, leave ya?"

"It looks that way, huh? All I know is she's not here."

"Well, I'm sorry." The corners of Rusty's mouth drop, and his eyes evade Dale's for a moment. "Did she give ya any warning or leave an explanation?"

"Nope."

"Well, any feelin' she's comin' back?"

"I'd say 'no.'"

"Geez," Rusty says, lifting his cap with one hand and running his fingers through what's left of his stringy black hair with the other, his gaze drifting toward the north before coming back to Dale. "Well, sorry ta hear 'bout all this, Dale. I was just thinkin' she was sick er sumpthin'."

"No worries."

"Say, how's that fridge treatin' ya?" Rusty sets his cap back on.

"Good. Good, ac'shally. Thanks."

"Well, I best be off," Rusty says, sticking out his hand. "Try not ta work too hard, Dale."

"I'll try," Dale says as they shake hands.

"Let me know if ya hear from her, alright?" Rusty says and starts to circle back around the truck.

"Sure thang," Dale says with a light wave of his hand before turning back to walk along the fence line. "Do I feel like she's comin' back?" Dale peers over his left shoulder to the south. "Right now, I don't feel nothin'."

SPOTLESS

Dale leans a cattle panel up against the new southwest corner post and the first of the new posts coming down the western fence line. He grabs the hammer and a barbed fence staple from the box atop the corner post. Dale straddles the panel's top corner with the staple at a 45-degree angle and drives it home.

Grabbing another staple from the box, he walks to the next post and the opposite corner of the cattle panel. The sky is a spotless Capri blue, the air still.

Dale hammers in the second staple and then looks up over the fence to see Amelia some 20 feet away, calmly chewing her cud, facing directly to the south. Dale keeps his focus on Amelia. "There's nothin' ta see out there, girl." Amelia flicks a fly from her ear and keeps chewing. "Just keep yur eyes on me. I'm all ya got."

Dale starts walking back to the corner post. "Hell, yur 'bout all I got too."

CALLOUSED

Dale strolls through a long alley of fencing materials behind Big R Fencing and Livestock Equipment. The sun is high and glinting off the metal racks of gating, cattle panels, and rolls of utility fencing. Warmth is emanating from the tightly packed dirt, the air stale and motionless.

"Hey, Dale, heard ya had a question," Len says as he approaches, right hand shielding his eyes, casting a shadow down the length of a red company polo.

"Yeah, I got a couple, I guess—What's wrong? Haven't been outside today?" Dale asks, coming to a stop.

"No, it's just bright out. It takes these ol' eyes more time ta adjust than it used ta. But I am more of an indoor cat these days."

"I'm just joshin' ya."

"Well, how can I help ya today?" Len asks, finally joining him.

"Well, I'm puttin' in a new fence, and I'm ready to start puttin' up some wire, and I was considerin' a few different options," Dale says, pivoting to look behind him.

"Like what? I can see yur checkin' out the different panels we have."

"Yeah, the ol' fence is all high tensile, but I was thinkin' a makin' the eastern side a bit stronger, cuz the wind blows all sorts a stuff inta the side, makin' it sag, and then some stuff gets through and piles up," Dale says, illustrating in the air with his hands. "But I know I can't afford doin' the whole thing in this stuff," he says, pointing to the nearest rack.

"Yeah, that stuff's gonna cost ya a pretty penny for the size a'property ya got. How big's yur lot?"

"Thirdy acres. But the main pasture's 'bout twenny."

"Well, yeah, that'll cost ya, but this here four-gauge wire will never have to be replaced," Len says, waving his pointer finger. "That's for sure."

"That's what I thought," Dale sighs.

"Ya sound a bit disappointed."

"Well, a fence that don't need fixin' don't need no one ta fix it."

"Most see that as a good thang, Dale," Len says, cocking his head. "That's kinda the point."

"Yeah, I know. But that sorta thing's just never felt right."

"Don't worry, there's always plenty a'work for a man ta do," Len says as he pats Dale's shoulder.

Dale glances up at the sun. "Speakin'a which, I best be gettin' along before I lose too much daylight."

"I hear ya." Len reciprocates with a quick peek but quickly blinks his way back down to Dale. "So how much'a these here cattle panels ya wantin'?"

"Well, if I'm gonna use it on one'a my long sides, I need enough ta cover 'bout fourteen hunnerd feet."

Len pulls out a calculator from his back pocket. "Alright, let me do some math here. If we divide fourteen hunnerd by sixteen-foot panels"—Len mutters half to himself—"we get ninedy, and ninedy at twenny-three dollars and fordy-nine cents equals—And I can give ya a bulk discount, which brings the total ta about twenny-one hunnerd dollars." Len directs his words back to Dale. "How does that sound?"

"If that's what it costs, that's what it costs."

"Alright then. Ya wanna come down and pick out the tensile wire ya want?" Len asks as he gestures for Dale to follow.

"I think I already know, but sure," Dale says and then steps in line with Len.

"Ya know, I admire yur ability ta work the land as hard as ya do, Dale. There's not many of ya left."

"I just do what I know, and hard work's nothin' ta be afraid of."

"That's true—and noble—but doesn't yur back ache? Don't yur hands hurt?"

"The hands, no."

"Let me see those mitts." Dale complies as they continue walking shoulder to shoulder. "Yeah, those things are callused, tough; it sorta reminds me a'the seasonal work I did back in my twennies. See, my uncle had a farm in Vale. Ya ever been there?"

"Yeah."

"Anyway, I used ta work out there with 'em for 'bout half the year, a little less maybe, and I always remember how bad my hands hurt at the beginnin'a every season, whether it be workin' the shovel or pushin' the wheelbarrow or whatever. And I remember rubbin' my hands at night those first few weeks," Len says, mimicking the way he used to drive his thumb deep into the palm of the other hand. "But sure enough, after a bit a time, my hands stopped hurtin', and by early fall, I had calluses just like that. Well, almost."

"I can't remember not usin' my hands."

"Oh, I bet. I bet. That's how it goes. We do sumpthin' for so long it becomes a part'a us, and we forget we weren't born ta dig holes and build fences and what-have-ya. We just get used ta it."

Dale looks past Len to the southern skyline. "Maybe some'a us are born ta."

"Maybe, Dale. Maybe."

Dale stops suddenly. "Oh, this here's the tensile I need."

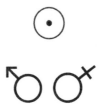

MISCARRIAGE

Dale stretches a strand of tensile wire taut, pins it to the post with the back of his left hand, and taps the staple in between his thumb and forefinger home with the hammer in his right hand. Thin, ashy clouds numb the weight of the morning sun, leaving the earth shadowless and cool to the touch, yet sweat still trickles down Dale's back inside his linen shirt.

Dale's eyes glance up to see his one pregnant heifer licking a dark spot on the ground some 50 yards away. He maneuvers through the old fence and starts walking toward her. She doesn't look up. His eyes are fixed on the dark spot as he approaches.

At ten paces away, he can make out the rudimentary shape of a squirrel-sized calf soaking in a garnet red pool. The heifer keeps licking the length of the tiny, motionless figure with a gentleness usually foreign to such a large clumsy tongue. "Goddamnit."

Dale circles to the rear of the animal to see long hanging globs of placental membrane. "That's what I thought." Dale softly steps back toward the heifer's head, pauses at her shoulder, takes the work glove off his right hand, and caresses her hair. She keeps up her rhythmic licking. "It's not yur fault, girl." He looks to a far-off hill where the horizon is a perforated edge of sagebrush. "It's none of our faults, is it?" Dale says, stooping down to inspect the aborted fetus. A few white lesions are visible. "Hmm. Well, I'm gonna let ya keep bein' a good momma for a few more minutes. Then I gotta getchya cleaned up and get rid of this—this thang."

Dale stands back up. "Goddamn you."

* * *

Dale lets the screen door snap shut behind him, wiping his boots at the sound of Janice's vacuuming. After a few passes of alternating dark and light lines, Janice notices Dale and flips the power switch off.

"I didn't know if ya'd cleaned the floor in here yet," Dale says, pointing to the kitchen and dining area, feet still planted on the welcome mat.

"Oh. No. Whatchya need?"

"Nothin' really. Just comin' to tell ya our one pregnant heifer just miscarried."

"Oh, poor thang. What a shame," Janice says, clicking the vacuum into its upright position.

"Yeah, it musta been the feed. Maybe some mold."

"Ya think so? How do ya know?"

"What else would it be?"

"I don't know. But aren't there other"—Janice beckons the air with her hands—"possibilities?"

"Yeah, there always are. But I'm use'ta stickin' with the first thought."

"Yeah, yur good at followin' yur instincts. I wish I was. It seems ta always pay off for ya."

"Yeah," Dale mumbles dryly as he pivots to go back outside. "I better get back ta the fence. Don't leave this door open too long."

"Okay. I'll have lunch ready when yur done."

Dale walks to the southern edge of the porch and scans the sky to see a few blue streaks making themselves visible. The vacuum hums through the screen door. "Maybe that's all I got."

REASON

A new, silver, Oregon State Police car pulls into Dale's gravel driveway. He sits on the shaded steps of his front porch, slicing chunks of apple with a small paring knife. The officer opens his door and steps out into the low-angled evening sun, pulling the brim of his campaign hat snug to his sun-glassed eyes.

"Good evening. You Dale Samuel?"

"I am."

"You got a minute? Can I have a word with you?"

"Yeah, why not?" Dale says, looking back down at his apple.

"I won't be long. I just have a few questions about your wife," the officer says as he shuts his car door and advances a few steps before stopping to loop his thumbs in his duty belt.

"And *you* are?"

"Excuse me?"

Dale lifts his head. "Who are ya?"

"Officer Dillon with the Oregon State Police. Glad to make your acquaintance." Dale puts a piece of apple in his mouth and chews, maintaining eye contact. "Alright. Were you aware that your wife has been listed as a missing person?" Officer Dillon asks, pulling out a notepad and pen.

"I am now," Dale says with a mouthful.

"Yeah, her boss over at A Taste of the Ranch—"

"Rusty."

"Yeah, that's right. Well, he filed the report. Said she hadn't been in to work for several days."

"Sounds 'bout right."

"What do you mean?"

"Well, she's been gone for several days, so I figure she's missed work too."

"Can I ask you why *you* didn't report her as missing?"

"Do husbands usually call the police when their wives, uh—"

"Leave?"

"Yeah."

"Well, do you know why she left? Or where she went?"

"Ya know, she didn't even leave a note."

"Didn't say anything?"

"Not about leavin'."

"Well, what did she say?"

"Whattaya mean?"

"Well, you said she didn't say anything about leaving, but did she say anything else to you?" Dale squints and tilts his head. "What was the last thing she said to you?"

"The last thang. The last thang," Dale says softly, his eyes wandering upward, scratching his chin with the butt-end of the knife. "I think the very last thang was my name."

"Your name?" Officer Dillon questions, before writing it down.

"Yeah."

"Dale."

"Yeah. And before that, I think she told me ta get some rest."

"Some rest?"

"Yeah, I gotta pretty good memory, but I can't claim that's word for word."

"Anything else you think might be helpful? Anything out of the ordinary?"

Dale shakes his head slowly. "Like I said, she didn't say nothin' 'bout leavin'. Maybe *she* didn't even know why."

"Hm, maybe. But usually, there's a pretty clear reason for someone disappearing, whether it's their choice or not."

"*Usually*, ya said?"

"Yeah, almost always."

"I reckon yur an expert on that."

"Well, us in law enforcement try to be. The only trick is sometimes you have to wait an awful long time to figure out what that reason is. But it's there, alright."

"Funny. I use'ta think the same thang."

Officer Dillon smiles and nods slowly. "I just have one more question for you."

"Go ahead."

"What was your wife wearing and driving, and all that kind of stuff, the last time you saw her? I'm afraid Rusty wasn't much help on that one."

Dale looks down at what's left of the apple in his hand, gently poking it with the knife. "She was wearin' a red and blue flannel, and her favorite pair of jeans—"

"Blue ones?"

"Yep. And she was in that li'l white Corsica."

"You know the year on that?"

"Niney-five."

"Well, Mr. Samuel," Officer Dillon says, pausing to finish scribbling down information. "I want to thank you for your cooperation."

"Sure. Anytime."

"Just give us a call if you think of anything else that might help." Officer Dillon then turns to leave.

"Will do, officer."

"Oh, just one more thing." Officer Dillon swings his car door open. "Just make sure to let us know if you're going to leave town for any reason."

HELPER

Dale pulls his truck up alongside the western edge of the pasture and puts it in park. There's barely any room to open the driver's side door, so he has to slither out and shuffle back to the left rear tire. "I didn't think'a that." Putting his left boot on top of the tire, Dale hoists himself up into the bed, careful not to catch his backside on the tensile wire.

The first five or so cows are already standing at the fence line. Dale picks up the pitchfork leaning against the other side of the bed, squares himself with a wide stance to the heap of alfalfa, and thrusts the tines into the middle of it. Dale first heaves directly to his right. Again, he thrusts and heaves, this time a little farther down the line. The bunch of alfalfa smacks right into the top row of tensile wire, causing it to disperse in a chaotic fashion. "Let's try that again."

Now, most of the herd is ambling over to the fence. Dale thrusts and heaves in the same direction, this time with such force that he almost trips over the wheel tub. "Woah." The alfalfa splays out softly on the other side. Again, he thrusts and heaves, this time a little farther up the line. This bunch of alfalfa spills over the back of a cow patiently waiting in line. "Goddamnit! Why don'tchya guys just—" Dale says, shaking his head. He then sets the pitchfork down and stares at the minimal space provided for him to climb back out of the pickup bed. "Ah, what the hell." Dale turns the opposite way and descends the other side of the truck. He opens the passenger door and climbs over the bench seat to the driver's side. With his left hand on the wheel and his right wrapped around the column gear shifter, Dale stares hard through the windshield to the southern horizon. "Ya know, yur not that big a help."

Dale then pulls the gear shift down to drive and eases forward ten or so yards along the uneven terrain, this time parking a few more feet from the fence line.

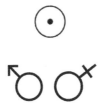

SUNRISES AND SUNSETS

Dale steps onto their back patio to find Janice's silhouette sipping a cup of tea and watching the sunset.

"It's beautiful, isn't it?" Janice asks without turning around.

"It sure is," Dale says, standing over her right shoulder.

"I suppose it's one thang I'll never get tired of."

"And why is that?"

The sound of slurping hot tea replaces an answer for a moment. "Because it's temporary."

"Hm," Dale says with a snort.

"Yeah. It's this fleetin' moment of brilliance, and if ya don't take the time ta look at it—or wait for it—you miss it. And every time ya do get the chance ta watch it slowly disappear, ya feel like ya witnessed somethin' special. Like somehow yur the only one who saw it. Of course, that's not the truth, but it feels like it is."

"Are all temporary thangs beautiful?"

"I don't know. I haven't thought about it like that before. But I know sunsets are. Maybe bein' temporary doesn't make 'em beautiful; it only makes 'em more beautiful."

Dale screws his eyes up at the western skyline. "So, if the sky was always orange and pink like that, ya think ya wouldn't find it quite so beautiful?"

"It's hard to say. Maybe. Maybe if the sky was always orange and pink, and only blue in the mornin' and at night, then that's what we'd sit and stare at."

"So, it's only the beginnin's and endin's of thangs that's beautiful?"

Janice turns to look at Dale for the first time. Dale's eyes remain fixed on the dissipating glow.

"Look, yur gonna miss it," Dale says without looking at her. Janice turns back toward the remnants of the sun. "It's kinda like what yur always sayin' about books. Startin' 'em and endin' 'em is the most excitin' part. The middle's just waitin'."

ESSENCE

Dale bends down to scoop up a New Hampshire Red in the midst of an evasive scamper. "Gotchya!" He cradles the hen in his left arm while working to secure both her legs with his right hand. "There we go." Dale hangs the hen upside down and, as she flaps her wings in a frenzy, walks around the corner and into the barn. "Easy there. Calm down." Dale's boots stop with a crunch of straw, and the hen submits, hanging stiff and still. "Ya know, when yur like this, ya remind me of a lot a people."

Dale slowly steps forward and lowers the hen into the killing cone. Turning over his left shoulder, he peers at the southern barn wall, then turns back around and looks down at his calloused hands. After a moment's pause, he shakes his head and grabs the knife off the table to his right. "Okay, girl. Let me just pull yur head down a li'l further," Dale says with his left hand securely around the chicken's neck. "There we go." He works his thumb over the base of her jawbone. "Okay." Holding firm with his left hand, Dale draws the knife up in his right and places it an inch above his thumb on the side of the hen's throat. "Here we go." Dale slices a quick but deep cut; the jugular instantly sprays down into a five-gallon plastic bucket. Dale tilts the neck away from the wound, and the blood turns into a steady stream of crimson. As the body begins to convulse inside the aluminum cone, he lets go of the neck and steps back. "That's what I like about ya. Ya keep fightin' even after ya lose. That takes guts. More guts than some of us at least." Dale turns back to look over his left shoulder and then down at the bloody knife in his hand.

* * *

Dale dips the headless body in the scalding pot by the feet and swirls it around in the 160-degree water. A few clockwise laps followed by a few counterclockwise, and then he pulls the dripping body out and tugs at a bunch of auburn feathers covering the thigh. Only half of them come out. "A few more seconds then," Dale says, submerging it back into the pot and repeating the same swirling motion. Pulling it out again, he tries a similar area on the other leg. This time they come out with ease. "Now that's more like it." Dale begins plucking the entire body, flicking wet feathers off his fingers into a bucket as he goes.

* * *

Dale plops the pale pink carcass onto an old blue and white gingham tablecloth, the feet still a bright yellow. "Now that's a—" Dale pauses abruptly and turns toward the far corner where several bones lie arranged on his work bench. "Hmm."

PLAYING GOD

"Hello," Dale says into the cordless phone.

"Hi. This is Dr. Marcoux from Sage Country Veterinarian Service returning your call. Is this Dale?"

"Oh, hi. Yes. How ya doin'?" Dale's boots thump on the kitchen linoleum.

"Good. Good. Now I understand you have some questions about artificial insemination for your herd?"

"Yeah, I'm afraid so."

"Why is that?" Dr. Marcoux asks. "You sound disappointed."

"I've just never had ta do it before. That's all." Caked on clods of dirt flake off with each step and powder the floor a dusty brown.

"Yeah, it can be quite the operation. May I ask why you're considering it now?"

"I basically haven't had any luck breedin' lately, and I figgered I oughtta try somethin' different," Dale says, turning heel-toe and heading into the living room.

"Fair enough. When were you looking at doing this?"

"As soon as possible."

"Well, let me see what's available," Dr. Marcoux says. "These types of services take some coordination on our end."

"I's actually figgerin' I could just buy the semen off ya guys and do the rest muhself." Dale strides across the brown carpeted room.

"Well, that's not really what we do here."

"Huh?"

"You see, Mr. Samuel, and I'm not trying to insult you or your operation here, but we have an obligation to make sure these types of products are used correctly and done in a safe and healthy way for the animals involved." Dr. Marcoux clears his throat. "It comes down to liability, really, and there's just too much of it tied up in this stuff for us to let you do it yourself."

"Hm." Dale pauses in the middle of the room. Loose dirt settles into the carpet.

"Does that make sense?"

"Yeah, I guess so."

"Do you still want me to check the schedule and see what's available?"

"Sure."

"Alright. It'll take just a second. Let's see here." Dale begins pacing as he listens to Dr. Marcoux flip through pages. "It looks like we could do next Thursday, actually. Does that work?"

"Uh, yeah. Yeah, let's do that."

"Alright, alright. Now let me just get down some basic information here."

"Okay."

"Where are you located?"

"I'm in between Riley and Hampton. 'Bout fifty miles from Burns. From yur direction, take a left on the dirt road before Highway Twenny bends northwest toward Hampton. Come down a li'l ways; ya can't miss it."

"Okay. How many cows do you have?"

"Thirdy."

"And will at least fifty percent of them be in heat by next Thursday?"

"Well, I'm not sure. But I thought ya could give 'em somethin' that would make 'em, how do ya say, sync up."

"You're thinking of prostaglandin and other estrus synchronization products," Dr. Marcoux says. "That would require a separate appointment and some patience on your end. We usually recommend researching what type of AI services are best for your herd ahead of time and giving it plenty of thought."

"Well, that's one thang I don't have time for now," Dale says, rubbing his belly and heading back into the kitchen.

"Okay, if that's the case, we can come out next Thursday and work on the cows that look ready, or you can take some time to think about this whole thing before going through with it."

"Let's do it next Thursday."

"Alright. What breed of cows do you have?"

"Herefords."

"All of them?"

"Yep. Well, all but one, but I'm not interested in breedin' her." Dale opens the refrigerator door.

"And how are you set up equipment-wise?" Dr. Marcoux asks. "Do you have enough chutes and things or a system set up to be able to service several animals rather quickly? Because we can bring out a sort of portable unit if necessary."

"Nah, I should have everythang we need." Dale surveys the desolate shelves. He spots a half-eaten steak wrapped in plastic and reaches for it.

"Okay. And what breed of semen do you want? I don't have Hereford."

"Black Angus, if ya got it, or whatever's the highest quality.

91

Ac'shally, it don't matter," Dale says, unwrapping the cold hunk of meat.

"Okay. And do you want me to walk through the prices for these services?"

"I'm not concerned 'bout the price, but sure." Dale bites into the steak.

"It's eighteen dollars per straw of semen. Then it's six dollars per cow the tech has to service. And then there's a flat fee of thirty dollars for coming out to you"—Dr. Marcoux pauses—"But that's for our area. And you're pretty far out there, so add on top of that, uh, I'll have to look up the exact amount, but you'll be charged for every mile we have to travel outside of Harney County. Do you want me to look that up real quick?"

"Nah, that's okay," Dale answers with his mouth full.

"So, does the rest of that sound alright to you?"

"It sounds fine."

"Do you have any other questions?"

"Well"—Dale forces himself to swallow—"just one, I guess."

"Alright. What is it?" Dr. Marcoux asks.

"What does it feel like?"

"Pardon me?"

"Creatin' life."

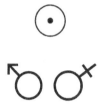

STILLNESS

Dale blinks once more at the ceiling and turns to see Janice still sleeping soundly, peacefully lying under the weight of a thick polyester blanket and a veil of moonlight wafting in through the window overhead.

With a sigh, he kicks his feet free and slides out of bed. "It's hot in here," Dale mutters to himself as he takes off his t-shirt. Shuffling in his underwear across surfaces of carpet and lino-leum, Dale opens each window wide and exchanges the back door's sliding glass for the screen. Then he positions himself in the center of the house: the transition between kitchen and living room. "Come on, breeze."

Dale waits.

Still nothing.

Dale rubs his calloused fingers against his calloused thumbs. The air doesn't move. He adjusts himself through his white briefs and walks out onto the front porch, careful not to wake Janice with the screen door. He locates the southern moon and faces it with palms to the cloudless sky, scraping the porch's dirt collected from one foot across the top of the other. Dale closes his eyes. "Where are ya? Where'd ya go? I can't feel nothin'."

Dale basks in stillness and moonlight.

No response. Nothing happens.

Dale lets his arms drop to his sides. His eyes open and start to scan the faintly discernible horizon. Back and forth.

He adjusts himself again. "Fine. If that's how it's gonna be. Who needs ya?" Dale barks before storming back inside, forgetting to keep the screen door from snapping shut.

* * *

"Dale, is that you?" Janice whispers with her eyes pressed shut.

"Yeah, it's me," he says with a hushed irritation still in his voice.

"Whatchya doin'?"

"Just openin' some windows. It got hot in here," Dale says, making his way to Janice's side of the bed.

"Oh."

"Ya mind if I open this one?"

Janice looks up to see Dale standing over her, skin gleamingly pale, a ghost against the surrounding darkness. "Sure," she says with a quick glance to the window above her head before closing her eyes again.

Dale carefully maneuvers his hand through the blinds, flips the lock, and slides the window open.

But there's no reprieve, just more stillness and more nothing. He looks down and studies Janice's profile for a moment. Her head turned away from him, her breathing slight. Dale runs his fingers along the grooves between his ribs, letting his left hand finally linger on the lowest one, sliding his thumb and forefinger back and forth, grabbing here and there. "With one a'these, huh?" Dale asks as he glances up to the window and then back down.

Janice stirs. "Ya comin' back ta bed?"

"Yeah," Dale answers, sliding his briefs to the floor. Drawing back the blanket and sheet reveals Janice's prone body inside an oversized cotton nighty. He throws his leg over hers and lies down on top of her. Janice groans under his weight.

"What time is it?"

"Don't know. Late or early, dependin' on how ya look at it."

"Are ya at least gonna kiss me?"

Dale's lips respond by faintly brushing hers, leaving Janice kissing air as he rears back to spread her legs and hoist the nighty up past the girth of her hips.

Dale lays himself back down, lowering hips, belly, then chest onto those of Janice. He looks at the corner of the pillowcase above her shoulder as he tries to find his way inside.

"Let me help," Janice says, reaching with her hand.

"I got it," Dale says. "There we go." He then begins to slowly thrust. Propping himself up with his arms, hands placed off the side of each of Janice's shoulders, he looks up at the window. Janice rubs her hands up and down his chest.

"I like it when—"

"Shh," Dale responds.

Dale stares at the window while Janice closes her eyes. He can see the moonlight coming through the blinds, but not the moon itself. He racks his focus to the blinds. They hang still and motionless.

"Come on!" Dale says jarringly against the steady cadence of their bodies clapping together; otherwise, the room is silent. Janice opens her eyes and furrows her brow for a moment. Dale's gaze remains fixed toward the window. She lets her hands fall to her sides, watching Dale until his eyes flutter. He stops thrusting and rolls over to his side of the bed.

"I guess yur finished," Janice says dryly.

Dale doesn't respond.

"Well, get some rest then," Janice says as she swings her legs over the side of the bed, cups her crotch with one hand, and waddles to the bathroom. Dale notices the blinds lightly swinging as Janice closes the bathroom door. A small grin forms across his face before he closes his eyes and drifts quickly to sleep.

Janice finds her way back to bed and blinks up at the ceiling for several minutes.

The blinds quickly regain their stillness.

PARTHENOGENESIS

Dale cracks an egg on the edge of the frying pan, splits it apart with both thumbs, then watches as the white splays out from the yolk and sizzles in the oil.

Grabbing another egg from the carton, he repeats the process, dropping the next wet mass on the other side of the pan. It sizzles and spits even more than the first as the oil pools to one side because of the lopsided burner.

Dale rotates the pan with his left hand and reaches for a third egg with his right before pausing. He double-takes then screws his eyes down to the second egg. "What the hell?" The faint outline of a beaked head is visible through the yolk. Dale grabs the spatula and jabs at the yolk with its corner to reveal the semblance of a wing and two feet. "Goddamn."

Dale turns to stare blankly out the window to the east, then rolls his eyes upward and cocks his head. "I've been grabbin' the eggs every day, haven't I? Then how'd this guy—" Dale asks, then trails off.

He then quickly opens the cabinet door under the sink and

dumps the entirety of the frying pan's contents in the trash. "Sorry, li'l buddy. I didn't know."

Dale reopens the cap to the vegetable oil and pours a small puddle into the center of the pan. "Let's try that again."

FORESAKEN

"Fuuuuck You!" Dale screams as his boots trample a row of yellow Oregon sunshine lining the edge of Janice's garden, shovel fully cocked behind his back. The flat side of the shovel then sledgehammers a squash plant. His right boot kicks at its mangled tentacle stems. "Fuck, shit, goddamn—" Dale golf-swings the shovel back and forth, chopping through squash and broccoli heads in rapid succession; his momentum spins him around haphazardly. "Fuckin' shit. Fuck, fuck, fuck—" The shovel blade gets tangled in a Medusa squash plant. "You motherfucker—" Dale struggles to yank it free with both hands, stumbles back a few steps through another broccoli plant, then takes a wild homerun swing at the cucumbers hanging from the A-frame trellis. "Ahhhhh!" His follow through makes him fall to one knee. "Fuck you, ya fuckin' shit fucker—" Dale pops back up onto two feet, turns the shovel's blade sideways up over his head, and crashes it down on the spine of the trellis. It cracks and splinters. "Fuuuuck!" He hammers down again. "Shiiiit!" He drives it straight down again. "Fuckin' goddamnit!" Finally, it breaks. Cucumbers and cantaloupe come sliding toward the trellis's compound fracture. Dale stomps the cucumbers and stems and leaves to the left with his right boot. "Fuck." And again. "Fuck." And again. "Fuck." Then he turns to the right and trounces the cucumber plants with his left boot. "Fuck. Fuck. Fuck." Stepping over the caved-in trellis, Dale takes aim at the cantaloupe. With a two-hand grip, he slams the shovel blade down from over his right shoulder onto a melon whose firmness and roundness cause it to squirt out to the side, relatively unscathed. "Goddamn you—" Dale spies another one, repeats the same motion, and this time the melon scoots the other way, scalped a bit but still whole. "Fuckin' piece a'shit—" Dale's third strike splits a cantaloupe right down the middle, but it hugs the shovel's blade. "Fuckin', get the fuck off ya—" He slams it down again. "Fuckin' piece a'shit." The melon is still stuck. Dale steps on it with his left boot and pries it free. "Fuck you!" He flings the shovel into a wire cage supporting a flimsy tomato plant. The shovel uproots the cage and careens into carrots and onions. "Take that ya fuckin' goddamn fuck—" Hands free, Dale plucks the next support cage and tosses it. "Piece a'shit." Then the next. "Fuckin' mother fucker." And the next. Flinging each one indiscriminately. On his way to retrieve the shovel, Dale kicks at the tops of carrots and onions. "Fuuuck!" Stomping on ones that escape sufficient tearing from the ground. "Fuck. Shit. Fuck." Dale stoops down to grab the shovel handle. Holding it vertically with both hands, he leans into it and pauses to take a series of deep, open-mouthed breaths.

Dale scans the part of the southern horizon not obstructed by the barn. Left and right. Back and forth. "*You* did this. Ya fuckin' sneak. Ya liar." Dale continues to scan. The landscape's brush stands tenuous yet still. "Still nothin', huh?" He surveys the tattered garden around his feet. "If this is how it's gonna be—" Dale hoists the shovel overhead once again and lines up the row of lettuce. "Ahhhhh!"

♂

DESEEDING

Dale stoops down at the long edge of Janice's garden with the Paiute seed jar in his left hand and a large, serrated kitchen knife in his right. He surveys the remnants of the once-orderly garden blanketed in long shadows cast by the early morning sun: smashed and whole vegetables strewn about, stalks bent flat across the ground, broken fragments of trellis, mangled wire cages, and shredded leaves.

He takes one squat step toward some whole tomatoes, sets the seed jar down, picks up a red sphere whose skin has maintained some of its tautness, and proceeds to slice it lengthwise.

Dale sets down the knife, extends his right forefinger, and digs it into the fleshy pulp of the tomato half in his left hand. Once he isolates an individual seed, he slowly slides it up to the lip of the tomato and pinches the seed between his thumb and forefinger. His hand hovers over to the opening of the seed jar, drops the seed inside, then slides his finger against the rim to detach the excess pulp. He then grabs the seed jar in his left hand, bringing it up to eye level. "This is where ya belong."

Dale gently sets the seed jar back down, picks up the same tomato half, and plunges his finger back into the pulp.

* * *

Dale presses his thumb down on the butt-end of a rotund squash seed, trying to pass through the opening of the seed jar. With a little more force, most of the seed squeezes inside, leaving some of its side meat on the rim. Dale flicks these remains off as he stands. "Yeah, I think that's 'bout all that'll fit."

Dale's eyes lift up from the seed jar and look over the dozens of halved tomatoes, cantaloupes, cucumbers, and squashes scattered in front of him, the brisk morning breeze washing over the nape of his neck. "I guess the cows'll get the rest a'ya."

* * *

Dale walks south from his property line, cupping the Paiute seed jar in his right hand, elbow clinging to his ribs, a shovel braced over his left shoulder. He maneuvers through big sagebrush and Idaho fescue without taking his eyes off the seed jar.

Dale pauses and turns back to look at his house, a mere pinky nail in the distance. "Alright. Gotta li'l ways ta go yet." He dabs his forehead on the sleeve of his right arm, careful not to knock off his hat.

He starts walking again and begins to hum. Cuts himself off, then begins again. Stops. "How'd that go again?" Dale asks, walking over bluebunch wheatgrass, eyes still glued to the seed jar. "Hm hm hm—nah, that ain't it. Hm-hm hm—ah, dammit. Hm hm hm-hm-hm hmm hm. There we go."

* * *

Dale cranes his neck around one more time as his boots come to rest in a relatively bare patch of dirt. He then looks right to the west and then left to the east. "Nothin', nowhere. This is the spot." Dale shuffles around a fixed point in the dirt till he's facing north, where his house ought to be. He sets the seed jar down to his right, flips the shovel from his left shoulder, and starts to dig.

* * *

Once the last shovel full of dirt is tossed on top of the seed jar and the hole is flush with the earth, Dale stands tall, letting sweat drip down between his shoulder blades inside his undershirt. He takes off his hat and lets the now faint breeze cool his wet hair, scanning the northern horizon left and right and left again. "Yeah, no one will bother ya out here. And no *thang*, neither."

JACKS

Dale studies irregular dingy-white shapes cupped in each glove as he staggers from his southern fence line. Each step of examination falls within the shaded halo of his full-brimmed hat. Little plumes of dust rise with each indentation, and the breeze carries it eastward. "I think I'll show Janice this time," he says, the corners of his mouth crawling upward. "These must be vertebrae. Janice'll say they look like they're from some ancient game'a jacks or somethin'."

Without looking up, Dale weaves through piles of back dirt from mini excavation sites: sporadic shallow holes seemingly blasted by buckshot from above.

Walking past the barn brings Janice's dismantled garden into view. Dale stops in his tracks. "Goddammit." His hands drop, but not before making fists to secure his findings. "How'd I forget?" Dale pivots to face the southern horizon; the breeze stiffens, forcing his eyes to squint. "So, is this what it's like? Bein' alone?" Dale takes a glance up at the high, piercing sun and a gust of wind hurls his hat along the ground behind him. Unflinchingly, Dale slowly tilts his gaze back to the horizon. "Well, it's not all it's cracked up ta be, is it?"

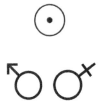

TELEOLOGY

Dale opens his eyes to the blue coolness of predawn light filling their bedroom. He turns his head toward Janice and up to the open window. The blinds hang still. Dale turns back toward the ceiling with a deep out-breath and begins tonguing his bottom row of teeth. His eyes survey the sprawl of spray sand texturing overhead, back and forth, as the lines and ridges become defined. Back and forth. "I suppose that's how we got here," Dale whispers to himself. "Part'a some big project. But each blob by itself don't matter much." He lifts his heavy hands from the bed and studies them. "But I did that with these." He slowly rotates at the wrists, inspecting his palms, then the backs of his hands, and then his palms again. Dale peeks at Janice sleeping, her chest rising and falling in a steady yet subtle cadence, and then back to his hands. "It's all I got," Dale whispers to himself with a nod.

Dale rolls on top of Janice, firmly placing a knee on either side of her waist. The jostling of the mattress and Dale's weight cause Janice's eyes to half open groggily. "What?

Again?" Dale thrusts his hands down on Janice's throat and leans in. "Dale—" Janice ekes out in a low guttural voice before Dale silences it with his tightening grip: thumb parallel to thumb, eyes fixed on the space between, fingers walking toward her spine from either side. Janice grabs Dale's forearms just above the wrist and tries to lift them up.

She's turning red now. Dale locks his elbows out and drives down, shoulders over hands. Janice tries to say something, but now her words are just a weak bubbling of spit. She starts kicking her legs and thrusting her hips, trying to buck Dale off. He cinches his knee-vice-grip even tighter. Janice's eyes are bulging; her face is now red-violet. Her fingernails dig into Dale's forearms. Dale keeps staring at his hands.

And then suddenly, her body goes limp. She stops kicking. Her hands slide off of Dale's and fall to the mattress. Her eyes roll back in her head.

Dale slowly releases his grip, rests his haunches down on Janice's midsection, and looks to the window. "Is that it? Now what?" The blinds gently sway as a breeze kicks up. Dale catches a stench; he points his nose around the room, searching for the source. He ends up craning his neck 150 degrees to spot, out of the corner of his eye, that the sheets are wet. He jerks his hips up and looks between his legs to see the vast stain of urine striped brown by the release of Janice's bowels. "Ah, goddamn."

Then a gasping attempt at breath escapes Janice's mouth as her jaw starts moving up and down, a fish lying on the hot sand, wheezing. "What the fuck?" Dale exclaims, noticing her eyes beginning to flutter. He glances at the window and then plunges both hands back down on Janice's throat before she becomes conscious enough to struggle. "Goddamnit, goddamnit, goddamnit," Dale spits out behind clenched teeth. "Fuck this shit." Dale drives all his weight down through her neck in surging motions until he hears some sort of cracking of cartilage or bone beneath his thumbs.

Janice's body lies motionless, but Dale keeps squeezing. The veins in his arms jutting out, face bright red, temples beginning to throb. Dale's hands feel something else give way in her throat, his fingers now touching at the back. "Come on. Come on," Dale chants in between deep breaths.

"Come on. Come on." Dale's hands begin to cramp.

"Come on. Come on." Janice's drooping eyelids cover all but tiny crescents of green irises.

"Come on. Come on." Dale's grip starts to weaken.

"Come on. Come on." Janice's mouth hangs frozen in the shape of a sigh.

* * *

Dale finally lets go, crawls off the bed, and stands beneath the open window, waiting for a cool reprieve. He stares at Janice's body while catching his breath and shaking out his hands.

After several minutes and no signs of life, Dale walks to the kitchen, pours himself a cold cup of coffee from the day before, and steps out onto the porch to witness the blooming sunrise. "Beginnin's and endin's, huh?"

♂

SOVEREIGNTY

Dale cuts the top row of tensile wire near the northwest corner of the old fence, the only section yet to be surrounded by the new. His leather-clad hand then squeezes the cutters around the next wire down, and then the next, and the next; each wire drops and coils a bit as the tension is relieved. Dale walks one post to the south and repeats the process. One by one, the stiff wires fall to the ground. He grabs the now-scraps of high-carbon steel and drags them out of the way, gesturing to the opened passage and the heap of dry hay that lies on the other side under a late evening sky being leached by the pale horizon. "Hey, come and get it!" A few cows start to amble over, and a few more ears perk up at the sound of his voice, but most remain speckled throughout the pasture. "That's it," Dale says as the first few cross over into the open. "Yur free ta go. Go on, get outta here."

* * *

Dale touches the rump of one of a dozen or so cows he has rounded up along the western fence line, his eyes on her firmly planted hind legs. "Come on. Tss-tss-tss," Dale says with a rattlesnake's cadence, stretching his arms into a T. "Get a move on. We're almost there. Tss-tss-tss."

At the hole in the fence, Dale's orderly platoon suddenly billows out and around an immobile, reddish-brown mass. "Woah, woah, woah." Dale halts and takes a couple steps back, arms still stretched wide. "Amelia, what's yur problem!?" Dale calls, then approaches her left flank. Her nose hovers at the very edge of the threshold. "What's wrong, girl?" I'm givin' ya all this. Enjoy," Dale says, gliding his hand back across the darkening horizon. Amelia stares straight ahead blankly. "It's okay." Dale inches closer and strokes her neck with the grain. "Ya can go...Listen, I know it's hard, but I'm doin' this for *you*. Don't worry 'bout me." Amelia simply shifts her weight a bit.

"Go on, get!" Dale begins to bark, pointing to the opening in the fence with his other hand. "Get!!" Dale shuffles toward her rear. "Come on! Tss-tss-tss. Let's go! Tss-tss-tss. Come on!" Dale says as he smacks Amelia's rump. She instantly kicks him, her hoof thumping his right thigh. Dale stumbles back, grabbing his leg. "Ahh! What the fuck ya do that for?"

No response.

"Come on, we're losin' light."

No response.

"Well, fuck ya, then," Dale turns and limps toward the house. "If yur not gone in the mornin'," he calls over his shoulder, "I'm gonna fuckin' kill ya!"

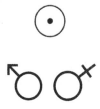

DOLLED UP

Dale cuts Janice's cotton nighty with a pair of her own sewing scissors from neckline to hemline, then, with the heels of his hands dug into the underside of her left hip, he rolls Janice's body onto her stomach with a two-handed heave. Dale wads up the filleted nighty and discards it in a black trash bag on the floor, then he folds the sheet over to cover the stain.

Dale circles the bed, grabs Janice's left ankle, and spreads her legs apart. Crawling onto the bed with his knees, Dale begins to wipe the insides of Janice's thighs with a damp washcloth. Folding the washcloth one time, he proceeds to wipe Janice's anus clean. He folds the washcloth once again, reducing it to a small, unsullied square. Dale then flips Janice back over by the hips and slowly wipes down her pelvic area and legs.

Dale dismounts the bed and tosses the soiled washcloth into the trash bag. He starts to pull the sheet toward him, bunching it into a ball as he gathers material, but then it pulls taut under the weight of Janice's body. Dale gives it a tug, but

Janice's limp body slides with the sheet. Dale gives it another tug; the force contorts Janice's upper body as the sheet breaks free under her legs. Dale lifts his bare left foot up and places it on Janice's right shoulder. With another tug, he pries the sheet free, rolls it up, and stuffs it in the black trash bag on his way to the foot of the bed.

Dale looks up from Janice's body to see the late morning sun starting to creep past their south-facing window. An angular beam spotlights the far corner of the room. Dale's feet follow his eyes to a shining patch of carpet. He wiggles his toes in the warm light. Then, stepping diagonally toward the window, Dale watches the beam crawl up his jeans. He stops when the thin rectangle of light settles on his bare chest. Dale runs his fingers through his chest hair as it coarsely diffuses the heat from his skin. He catches his reflection in Janice's vanity slightly to his right, looks at himself, looks at Janice's body to his slight left, forming a backward lowercase R, and then straight ahead to the window. Lifting his arms out for a wide embrace, Dale tilts his head back, closes his eyes, and takes in a deep breath through his nose. Then an out-breath. Then another in-breath.

After several deep breaths and as the ray of sun starts to slide off his left shoulder, Dale opens his eyes, lowers his arms, and squares himself to the bed. "Whatta ya wearin' today, Janice?"

* * *

"Alright. Let's getchya dressed," Dale says, setting down a fully packed duffel bag and tossing a pile of clothes on the bed next to Janice's body. "We're goin' for a drive later tonight."

Dale climbs on the bed, knees first, and grabs Janice by the arm. His hands recoil from the iciness of her pale skin. "Geez!" Then he reclaims his grip, pulling her from her bent position into a straight line. "Gosh, yur gettin' stiff already. We better do this quick."

Dale grabs a pair of faded pink cotton panties. "Now, let's get these on," he says, slipping them over her feet. "And I promise not ta complain 'bout ya not wearin' sexy underwear." One corner of Dale's mouth curls up in a crooked smile as he slides the panties up to the widest part of Janice's thighs. "Alright now. Let's getchyur legs together." Dale straddles Janice's prone legs and squeezes them together with his knees. "Okay, here's the tough part. Can ya just—" Dale grabs the waistband on the underside of either leg and tries to lift the hips up and slide the panties into position in one swift motion. "Ah, there ya go. Wooh!" Dale exhales, gently adjusting the waistband below Janice's belly button.

"Alright. Let me grab this bra," Dale says, reaching to his right. "Now, I know this all would be much easier without this, but, like ya say: 'Ya can't leave home with 'em flappin' 'round for the whole world ta see,'" Dale says, arranging the dingy, off-white bra in front of him, so it's facing the right way. "Now, let's put yur arm through here. And then the other." Janice's arms lie stiffly at her sides, so Dale cuffs her hands loosely, one bra strap at a time. Then he works the straps up to her shoulders, scooting his knees forward on the bed as he does so.

Climbing to the side of Janice, Dale scoops a hand under her shoulder blade, the other at the small of her back, and flips her over so she lies face down again. Dale brushes her hair to the side, then reaches for the straps and readjusts them so they lie flat and snug over her shoulders. His hands slide down and work at the back. "These I's never real good at." Dale turns his head sideways, leans down close to his hands, and guides each hook into its rightful eye closure. "Got it."

Dale sits back on his haunches, takes a deep breath, and picks up a red and blue flannel shirt. "While yur like this, I'm gonna get this started." Dale holds the shirt up by the collar, then lowers it and begins enveloping Janice's right arm with the sleeve until the hand slides through the cuff. Dale then slings his left leg over to straddle Janice again as he tries to stretch the opening of the left sleeve to Janice's left hand. "Damn. Not enough slack." Dale lowers the sleeve off the right shoulder a few inches and tries again. "There we go," he says, pulling the collar up to the nape of Janice's neck.

Dale stands up, back curled. "Now, let's see if I can flip ya over like this." Dale grabs Janice's left shoulder and bicep and tugs her over to her back again, her legs left twisted at the ankles. Dale lowers himself back to a mounted position. "Oops." Janice's left breast droops out of the cup. "I gotchya." Dale pulls the bra out with his left hand and lifts the breast into place with his right. "Now, let's button ya up." Dale brings the two sides of the shirt together at the second button, then sweeps Janice's hair clear with the back of his hand, revealing a dark purple band around her throat, growing in contrast to her now-porcelain skin. Dale pauses, looks at his hands, then glances up at the window. Then he goes to work on the second button, fitting it through the hole. Then he buttons the third. And the fourth. The fifth. Sixth. Seventh.

"Yu'll be glad ta know I grabbed yur favorite jeans," Dale says as he reaches over for them. "I'm hopin' that means they're easy ta put on."

Dale scoots backward off the bed, uncrosses Janice's legs so they lie parallel, and then slides the waistband over her feet and up to her shins. One leg at a time, Dale bunches the jeans up on her lower legs until the hem passes the ankle.

Dale remounts the bed, hovers his hips over Janice's knees, reaches back through to secure the waistband, and yanks it up over her knees. Dale knee-waddles up the length of Janice's body until his hands are again under his hips and yanks again. This time the jeans stick on the girth of her hips. Dale waddles up a bit. "Okay, here we go again." Dale slides his right hand to the backside of the jeans as his left hand reaches over to lift the hip. In two conjoined motions, Dale tries to pull the jeans up over Janice's left buttock. Lift and jerk. Lift and jerk. Lift and jerk. "Got it! Whew! Okay. Now let's just zip ya up."

Dale dismounts the bed and grabs a pair of socks and shoes. As he adorns her feet locked at 90-degree angles, Dale looks over Janice's body. Then he looks up to the window. "It's strange. She already doesn't look like Janice." Dale's eyes come down to Janice's left shoe to help secure the double knot. Then he ties the right one. "Well, Janice, I best get outside." He finishes another double knot. "I'll see ya tonight."

SUBVERSION

Dale drives the blade of a round-nose shovel into a small crater growing in the northwest section of his pasture. A gale billows through his shirt and tugs hard at the brim of his hat, forcing him to stop and secure it with his left palm pressed flat atop his head. "There's no use tryin' ta dig with this thang on," Dale says, taking off his hat and coiling it in the nook of his arm, ready for a toss. The gusts flip up what hairs are not wetted and stuck to his scalp. "Ah, forget it." Dale lets the shovel handle drop and sets off toward the house.

As Dale marches past the barn, a dark fluttering mass catches his eye over his right shoulder. He stops to see a massive golden eagle severing the spinal cord of one of his few black Australorps. "Oh, my—" Dale mutters. The eagle spreads and flaps its wings to steady itself in the wind. Dale stands, mouth agape, before coming to. "Hey!" The eagle looks up. Dale steps toward it and waves his arms over his head, his left hand still grasping his hat. "Get outta here! Go on! Leave my chickens alone, ya goddamn—" Dale pauses and looks south over his right shoulder. A mix of white and light gray clouds scurry and stretch east, making it hard to discern the exact horizon line.

Dale turns back to the eagle as it sinks its talons deeper into the body of the chicken. "Hey!" He continues waving his arms and stepping forward. "I'm not scared'a you!" The eagle cocks his head at Dale, lets out three high-pitched wips, and takes off in a flurry of brown and black feathers, still clutching its kill. Dale recoils, shielding his face with his hat as its wings flap overhead.

Dale doesn't watch the eagle fly away. Instead, he takes a quick peek to the south and then pivots toward the dozen or so feathers being blown about in front of the coop where his chicken used to be. He takes a few more steps forward and then toes some feathers with his boot that are stuck to the dirt with blood. "Heck, birds like that are suppose'ta be scared'a you black ones."

Dale bends over to pick up a long brown feather that dwarfs the others. "But I suppose this ol' eagle got too smart for that trick." Dale turns his head to the south, but the side of the barn is all he can see. "Yur not playin' by the rules," he says as his eyes drift up to the passing clouds.

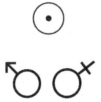

THE BLUE HOUR

Dale eases off the gas as the Corsica's steering wheel starts to shimmy. "Woah. Didn't re'lize I's goin' that fast. Definitely don't wanna get pulled over tonight." Dale glances at the rear-view mirror to see a long stretch of twilight-kissed highway under a cobalt sky. Through the windshield, dark sapphire fades into a black indecipherable horizon. The headlights faintly illuminate a mere hundred yards of speeding asphalt at a time.

"Thangs are gonna be different now," Dale says, quickly craning his neck toward the passenger side window. "That's for sure." He snaps his eyes back to the road, down to the trip meter momentarily, and then back to another straightaway, his left hand casually draped over the wheel.

"Janice, this reminds me a'how ya'd always fall asleep on road trips. For some reason, though, it use'ta make me feel more lonesome than when I's by muhself. Like the idea of not bein' listened to, or sumpthin'. Maybe *you* know how that feels." Dale takes a quick look to his right again, squinting at the horizon line. "But I guess ya'd tell me I didn't say much worth listenin' to."

His eyes come forward and spot headlights crawling up over a gentle rise. "This is the first car I've seen in a long while." Dale places his hands at ten and two and guides the car slightly away from the centerline. As the car approaches, Dale locks his focus on a point in his lane about two car lengths ahead while he's temporarily blinded by the passing lights. He then immediately starts scanning the right side of the road.

"It's comin' up here quick." Dale lets off the gas, then checks the rearview mirror. "I swear it's right around here." Feathering the gas pedal, he looks down at the trip meter again. "Is this it? Yep." Dale brings the car to a stop on the highway, making sure the sign reads "OO Ranch Rd." He looks back up to the rearview mirror and then straight out in front of him. "All clear." He turns south over the jarring vibration of a cattle guard, followed by the steady crunching of road mix. "Moon Reservoir, here we come."

FREE WILL

Dale marches into the pasture as he slides 4-shot shells into the magazine of his 12-gauge shotgun. The early morning sun is still a soft gold; a brisk westerly breeze sweeps across isolated tufts of desert grass. Amelia stands in the far end of the pasture, nose pointed southeast, opposite the freshly cut hole in the fence.

Dale circles in front of her, squaring to the north and pumping a shell into the chamber. "I told ya ta go." Dale holds the gun diagonally across his chest. "This is yur last chance." Amelia's jaw works lazily over some cud. "And ta think'a all I done for ya," Dale says, setting the buttstock to his shoulder. "I offered ya a new life. And ya didn't take it."

Dale aims the barrel at Amelia's right front shoulder, closes his left eye, and fires. The pasture erupts a cloud of birds. Amelia stumbles back and falls on her left side. A wide hole instantly gushes, sending dark tributaries through her tawny hair. Amelia rears her head toward her shoulder repeatedly as her legs furiously work to get themselves under her bulking mass.

Dale pumps another shell into the chamber and takes a step toward her broad side. Amelia manages to stand up, but as she puts her weight on her right front foot, the leg buckles. She stumbles forward, stops her momentum with her good front leg, and balances tentatively, her jagged crater of a wound oozing. She looks at Dale and snorts as her tail begins swishing rapidly.

Dale takes aim and fires a second shot that explodes Amelia's left front knee. Her chest crumples straight to the ground, landing on a bloody nub still clinging to her lower leg by a mere shred of hide. Amelia lets out a high-pitched bawl, and then another, and then another; her back legs shuffle awkwardly, driving her nose into the dusty earth.

Dale pumps the shotgun again, stepping closer. Finally, Amelia's back legs resign and fold themselves up under her girth as she bawls wildly. Dale takes another step forward and blasts a third shot through the soft tissue of her flank. Mangled hunks of purple-brown innards launch from a gaping exit wound and paint the ground in a crimson shower. The shot turns Amelia on her side, slowly writhing in a quickly widening pool of burnt umber mud. Her bawls dissipate into a soft guttural whine.

Dale walks toward Amelia's head, boots displacing the wet sticky earth, slurping on each up-step. "Go on and shut up already!" Dale kicks her in the throat, gun hanging low across his thighs. Amelia flinches and recoils, but only her head and neck move. Her limbs now lie flaccidly. She continues her whining incantation. Dale kicks her again. "I said shut up!" Her upward eye is locked on Dale. Amelia's breathing slows as her blood-soaked body sags into the earth, her neck bowed into a contorted arc. Her whine finally whimpers, sputters, and stops.

Dale kneels down close. Amelia blinks slowly but keeps her focus on Dale as he turns his ear and leans in further. A faint gurgling sound can be heard, and a mix of blood and snot and dirt slowly bubbles from her nostrils. "Well, I'll be damned," Dale says, standing up. "Yur one tough cookie."

Dale raises the butt back to his shoulder and hovers the barrel over Amelia's face until their eye contact is broken. "You made me do this."

He pulls the trigger. The thundering echoes dissipate quickly into the morning breeze.

BREATH OF LIFE

Dale swings open the front door to Sewell's Taxidermy with his left hand and spins backward into the showroom, a rolled-up towel pinned under his right armpit and a plastic grocery bag dangling from his hand. He is instantly greeted by the blank stare of a few dozen elk, mule deer, and pronghorn antelope heads and necks seemingly growing out of the wall. Dale scans the pronghorns as he steps further inside.

"Oh, hi! How ya doin'?" asks a blond woman returning from the back with a thin stack of papers.

"Pretty good, I guess," answers Dale.

"What can I help ya with?" She sets her paperwork aside and hoists her form-fitting jeans by the belt loops, hips wriggling back and forth.

"Well, I—I was hopin' to—" Dale starts and stops, still looking at the animal heads more than her. "Doesn't a man do all this?" Dale sweeps his free hand toward the rows of heads.

Her lips purse. "Yes, my husband does, but I'm sure I can help ya," she says, with hands folded neatly on the counter.

"Can he do that all by himself?"

"They are beautiful, aren't they?" she admits, glancing over her left shoulder. "But he doesn't have to. This is a family business. Everyone has an important job to do."

"I bet. But he's the one that gets 'em ta look like that, right?"

"With a li'l help, yes," she says with a nod and only a thin trace of a smile. Then she presses her palms flat on the counter and shifts her weight onto one leg, the other foot dotting the *i* behind her. "Now why don'tchya bring over whatever it is ya got there, and we'll see what we can do for ya."

"Alright." Dale steps all the way up to the plywood counter, grabs the grocery bag with his left hand, and sets it down gently. The contents make a hollow clank as they shift inside. "This here's the big stuff." Then Dale sets the towel down and slowly unrolls it to reveal several small bones. "And these are the li'l guys."

"Oh, wow." She leans over to inspect them, brushing her long ponytail back over her shoulder. "Do ya mind if I touch 'em?"

"Nah, go right on ahead," Dale says, rummaging inside the plastic bag. "Just be careful."

"Of course." She turns a small bone over in her fingers. Dale lifts out a slender skull with large canines, one twisted capital *F* of an antler, and a few straight, long bones and sets them alongside each other on the towel.

"Can ya guys mount this skeleton?"

She stands up quickly, furrows her brow, and blinks several times as her vision pans across Dale's collection. "Uh, well—that's not really what we do here. Plus, if ya don't mind me askin', what is it?"

"It's mine."

"Okay. Well, it looks like ya got bones from several different animals." She pauses and looks at Dale. His arms are folded across his chest. "Yeah, this antler is definitely mule deer. This skull looks to me like a coyote or sumpthin'. Ya can tell by these," she says, running her index finger along a row of teeth. "And the rest'a these are probably a mix'a thangs."

"So ya can't do it?"

"I'm afraid not, sir," she says, shaking her head and puffing her cheeks into a smile.

"I see." Dale starts to put the larger items back into the plastic bag.

"But if yur really serious about it, the people at the High Desert Museum over in Bend could probly help ya out." Dale nods as he begins to roll the towel back up. "But from what I hear, a lot a people are just doin' that kind'a stuff by themselves nowadays. Yeah, I think there's a lot'a stuff on You-Tube."

"You tube?" Dale asks, placing the rolled-up towel back under his right arm.

"Never mind." She waves her hand back and forth. "Let me just give ya our card, and ya let us know anytime we can help ya out with one of our traditional services. I'm Renee, by the way," she says, pointing to her name on the card.

Dale grabs the grocery bag and then clamps down on the card with his free fingers. "How does it feel?"

"Pardon me?"

"How does it feel to make all these dead thangs seem so alive again?"

"It feels great," Renee beams. "Makin' people happy is what we're here for."

"Huh," Dale snorts. "Ain't that the truth. Well, I reckon I'll get outta yur hair." He turns to leave.

"Thanks for comin' in. It was nice ta meetchya."

"Tell your husband I admire his work."

* * *

Dale squints at the signage of each aisle at the Dollar Tree as he passes by, pausing briefly at each intersection. The nasal voice of a sales associate interrupts his surveying. "Can I help you with something?" Dale's boots squeal as he turns heel-toe on the linoleum.

"Yeah, where do ya keep the Super Glue and the wire hangers?"

"All our hangers are plastic, I think, but the Super Glue is over here on aisle five."

* * *

Dale sets a bottle of Super Glue, some needle-nose pliers, and several wire hangers on Janice's sewing table next to the plastic grocery bag and rolled-up towel full of bones. A wadded-up bundle of extra tensile wire lies on the floor. Dale clicks on a desk lamp and takes a seat.

He slowly unrolls the towel and widens the opening of the bag with the backs of his hands. He then turns to uncap the glue and begins untwisting the neck of a hanger. Looking left toward the window, his reflection can vaguely be seen against the darkening night. Dale studies his image for a moment. He turns back to his work once the hanger in his hands is straight. "Alright, let's begin."

* * *

A rooster signals dawn three times with haggard crows. Dale unhooks a hanging basket of English ivy, descends a footstool, and sets the plant down on the brown carpet. He then steps over to the couch and slowly lifts an obtuse A-framed piece of wire acting as a marionette's control bar for the skeleton dangling from filaments of thread and fishing line. Dale corrals the figure with his free hand and keeps the supporting strings from tangling. In this manner, he steps back up on the stool, raises the wire, and sets the makeshift mobile on the hook. "There ya are."

Dale steps back down, retreats to the center of the room, eyes fixed on his creation, and smiles. The one antlered coyote skull hangs heavy and limp. The two finished legs help counterbalance the weight. The body that joins them is an incomplete connect-the-dots of miscellaneous bones. "Yeah, that's good."

CONCUPISCENCE

Dale pulls the white Chevy Corsica off of Moon Reservoir Silver Creek Road, where it runs closest to the deep, most northern water, its high beams shining on what appears to be a smooth, black vacancy of sage and tall grass.

Dale turns off the lights and steps out of the car. Moving a few paces toward the shore, the sound of the water lapping replaces that of the idling engine. The moon spreads a soft blue film over the breadth of the landscape's texture, ceasing the need for synthetic light. "This'll do," Dale says.

Dale walks back to the car and reverses it onto the road in a perpendicular fashion, nearly enveloping the width of the narrow strip of asphalt. "These wheels'll need ta start with some grip." He pulls the parking brake, then pops the trunk and walks around to unload a wool blanket and some firewood, tossing them behind the car. Lastly, he grabs two bricks and sets them down on the road with a heavy clack.

Dale approaches the passenger's side and opens the door. "Okay, Janice, it's yur turn ta drive." He reaches across her waist and releases the seatbelt. "I'm just gonna grab ya under here," Dale says as he grunts. He lifts her from under her armpits, pulls her toward his chest, then wrestles and contorts her stiffened body until her legs untangle themselves from the car entirely. Dale lets her lower half rest on the ground for a moment. "This is harder than birthin' a calf. Alright, here we go," Dale manages to say between clenched teeth as he hoists her off the ground and drags her all the way around the car, heels bumping along the pavement.

He manages to shove her into the driver's seat, her back to the center console. "Now let's get yur legs in," Dale says, maneuvering the rigid lower limbs in one at a time. "Let's scoot ya in the center. There, that oughtta do it." Then, from outside the car, Dale steps in with his right foot to press the brake, then, supporting himself with the steering wheel in his left hand, he reaches over to put the car into drive with his right. Dale takes his foot off the brake, and the parking brake holds.

Dale picks up the two bricks as he circles back to the passenger's side. He stretches himself across the seat to lay the first brick on the gas pedal. The engine revs to a whine. Dale lifts his head up and checks the tachometer. "Let's add this one right here," Dale says, leaning the second brick on the first to apply more pressure. The engine strains a few octaves higher. "Now, let's see if we can just put yur foot here, Janice. To brace it. Alright," Dale says, working his way onto his knees in the passenger's seat. "We kinda gotta hurry, but let me see ya one last time under the stars and moon." Dale switches off the dome light. "I had ta do this, Janice. To—to find out. Don't take it personal." He tucks a strand of hair behind her ear, leans forward, and kisses her icy, colorless lips. "Goodbye."

And with that, Dale puts his feet down outside the car as far as he can reach, releases the parking brake, and jumps back quick to watch the car speed toward the reservoir. It veers a little left, kicking up dirt, but avoids any thick shrubs.

The car enters the water with a muffled roar of a splash. The tires churn, and the exhaust spits until the nose points down and the engine is suffocated. Dale follows the car's path at a jog. Waves slap at the gentle slope of the shoreline. The car sinks slowly, teasing Dale with little lurches where it appears to be prematurely striking bottom. "Keep goin'," Dale pleads. "Be deep enough." At last, the reservoir swallows the car. The waves soften and gather more distance between them. With a deep sigh, Dale turns back toward the road.

Just off the asphalt's edge, Dale stoops down to load his arms with firewood. Upon standing, Dale looks back at the water quietly working toward stillness and then up slightly to the horizon. "This better work."

REVELATION

Dale dangles his legs over the edge of Abert Rim. A high Naples-yellow sun makes a thousand little jewels of the brine-tinted lake more than 2,000 feet below. The peeps, chirps, and whiny grunts of a waterfowl symphony are suddenly muffled by the advancing crunch of boots from Sergeant Quinn and two accompanying officers. Dale picks apart a white sulfur flower. His shotgun lies across his lap.

"Dale Samuel?" Sergeant Quinn asks, trying to gather his breath, hands on his hips.

"Yeah."

"I'm Sergeant Quinn of the Oregon State Police Department. This here's Officer Dillon, who I think you've already met, and Officer Ackerman."

"It don't make no sense," Dale says without turning around.

"What doesn't?" Sergeant Quinn asks as he raises two outstretched palms. The other two officers stop advancing.

"A lake with no fish."

"Huh?"

"That lake down there. Fish can't live in it. Too salty."

"Oh. Well, those shorebirds sure love it." Sergeant Quinn comes to a stop, his right hand on his sidearm.

"Yeah, but they're only migratin'. They don't live here."

"Well, I guess that's true."

"I mean, who'd think a such a thang? What's the point?" Dale asks, tossing white bits of flower over the edge.

"Hmm. Well, she's beautiful, ain't she? People are comin' up here all the time to take her in. As long as they can handle that hike comin' up here. Ain't that right, boys?" Sergeant Quinn chuckles, glancing quickly over each shoulder, his jowls flapping side to side.

"There's gotta be more to it than that."

"Maybe. Maybe you're right." Sergeant Quinn lifts his sunglasses with his left hand and scans the horizon. A congregation of snowy plovers flutters into the air.

"The problem is, it'll be all dried up before we figger out the answer. And people don't need answers for thangs that no longer exist. Or maybe they do, and that's the point. I don't know. I haven't figgered that part out yet." Dale throws what's left of the flower down past his feet.

Silence hangs for a moment. "Dale, do you know why we're here?"

"Now that's the million-dollar question." Dale's hands come to rest on the barrel and buttstock of his shotgun.

"Now hold it right there!" Sergeant Quinn barks; he and the other officers draw their weapons. "Let go of the gun!"

"Don't worry, Sarge. I won't shoot nobody. I already know it won't change nothin'," Dale says, slowly pulling the gun up over his head.

Sergeant Quinn holsters his sidearm and approaches slowly. "Is it loaded?"

"Yeah. But the safety's on."

"Okay, just keep her steady." Sergeant Quinn grabs the middle of the gun with his left hand and takes two quick steps back. "Here, Dillon. Take it," he says, holding it out to the side, eyes on Dale. Officer Dillon complies. "Now, can I have you get up real nice and slow?"

"Ah, I reckon." Dale scoots back from the ledge and stands up, still facing the lake.

"Now hands on top of your head," Sergeant Quinn asks, reaching for his cuffs. "Okay, now step back towards me, please." He grabs Dale's left hand, pulls it behind his back, turns the palm out, and slaps on the first cuff. Repeating the process with the right hand, Sergeant Quinn asks, "Why'd you do it, Dale? Why'd you kill your wife?"

Dale looks up for a moment and then back down. "Because I wanted to understand."

VIRGA

Dale's right forefinger slides across the spines of Janice's shelved novels as thunder growls to life outside. He cocks his head and looks to the window, waiting for a flash of lightning. The wind picks up as the tree branches whoosh and the house's frame groans. Then a flicker illuminates the clouds outside, sending Dale bursting through the house and out the front door.

A sudden clap of thunder sounds just as Dale descends the porch steps, catching him mid-stride; he momentarily cowers, then proceeds down his driveway with swift gravel-crunching steps. Dale turns his palms to the sky as he walks. "Hm, no rain."

Dale reaches the road. The next lightning strike explodes in the sky just southwest of the pasture to reveal a thick cotton canopy hugging close to the desert floor before all returns to a darkness faintly lit by a gibbous moon. "Is that all ya got?" The wind surges, and Dale begins to trot down the road to the south.

Thunder booms and stops Dale in his tracks, wide-legged. He looks up, and his eyes flit back and forth. Cloud to cloud lightning strikes again, right over the southern fence line. "Come and get me ya fuckin' pussy!" Dale screams into the night sky, then pries his shirt up over his head. "I'm right here," he says, beating his bare chest with his fist, still stomping down the road, dust blowing against his skin.

This time the lightning strikes sideways, just to Dale's right, and before he can look up, thunder seemingly splits the sky in two. Dale tilts his head back, closes his eyes, stretches his arms as wide as he can, and waits.

Seconds pass.

Then another flash and crack, this time simultaneous and directly overhead. Dale opens his eyes. "Ya can't hurt me, can ya?" His mouth falls into a wide, toothy grin. His gaze follows a spot in the darkness above as it drifts over his left shoulder. At the same time, Dale's right hand rises above his head, index finger extended, tracing his eyes' point of focus.

The next lightning flashes a mere inch from the tip of Dale's finger, and, after a split-second delay, Dale flicks his wrist, and therefore his finger, in the direction of that lightning flash's origin. "Almost got it," Dale says softly.

"One, one thousand," Dale mutters, then flicks his wrist in perfect anticipation of the next lightning strike. Dale erupts in laughter. "Yes!" His feet pivot to fully face the east.

"One, one thousand, two—" Dale flicks his wrist and barely mistimes the next strike.

"One, one thousand; two, one thou—" Another near-perfect timing. "Haha! Who needs ya?!?"

With that, Dale raises his left index finger to match his right, the wind still howling at his back. As he widens his vision, he notices the abundance of pulses littering the expansive sky. The toothy grin returns to Dale's face as both hands commence intermittently tapping at the sky.

⚤♂

APOTHEOSIS

Sergeant Quinn's silver patrol car cruises north, hugging the subtle undulation of Highway 395 under a fluorescent canopy of summer sun. Dale sits cuffed in the backseat, humming softly to himself. Sergeant Quinn looks up at Dale in the rearview mirror to see his gaze oscillating from side window to side window and back again, all while carrying the same tune.

"Whatchya hummin'?" Dale doesn't respond. "Dale! I said, 'whatchya hummin'?'"

"Oh, nothin'. Just some ol' Patsy Cline," Dale says before hopping right back on beat. "Hm-hm hmm hm—"

"Well, how does it go?"

"Hm hm hm hm-hm—I don't know all the words. Janice did, though. Hm-hm hm hm hm hmmm—"

"One of her favorites?"

"Yeah, it was. Hm hm-hm hm hm hmm—"

Sergeant Quinn scans the landscape slowly from left to right, checks the rearview mirror, then speaks over his shoulder, "You seem pretty happy. You know, for a guy in your position."

Dale pauses his humming and scooches forward in the seat, inching close to the grated partition. "It's cuz I'm finally free."

"What the hell are you talkin' about?" Sergeant Quinn scrunches up his face into little deltas of wrinkles. You're gonna be locked up for a long time. Most people think of that as the opposite of freedom."

"I know. I know. But most people haven't"—Dale's eyes drift toward the roof of the car as he trails off—"done what I've done, I guess."

"Thank goodness for that," Sergeant Quinn chuckles. "We don't need any more murderers around here."

"That's not what I mean. I, uh—I—forget it," Dale says, slouching back in the seat. "But there's a certain kind of freedom in bein' locked up." Dale tries to scratch his ear with his shoulder. "It's hard to understand. It's harder to explain."

"I bet."

"What I suppose I mean is: I don't have ta think about it no more." Dale's lips curl into a faint grin.

"Yeah, guilt can eat a man up."

"That's not it." Dale's grin flattens as he shakes his head.

"What is it, then?"

"Everythang else."

The near silence of white road noise hangs in the air. Dale begins to hum again.

"Dale?"

"Yeah."

"Are you a God-fearin' man?" Sergeant Quinn asks with screwed-up eyes and a furrowed brow.

"I reckon I use'ta be." Dale scoots back up to the front edge of the seat. "But I suggest ya don't spend too much time thinkin' 'bout such thangs."

"And why is that?"

"Cuz that's how it starts."

"Huh?"

"Let's just say it'll save ya a lot'a trouble," Dale says as he gently rolls back into the seat. "Trust me. It'll save you all a lot'a trouble."

Sergeant Quinn flits his eyes back and forth between the road and the rearview mirror. Dale starts to faintly sing.

"Pick me up when dreams are shattered,

When false friends cannot be found,"

"Dale."

"For you know I'll still be waiting,"

"Dale?"

"Pick me up on your way down."

"Coulda, woulda, shoulda."

What you don't understand you can make mean anything.

— Chuck Palahniuk, *Diary*

ABOUT ATMOSPHERE PRESS

Atmosphere Press is an independent, full-service publisher for excellent books in all genres and for all audiences. Learn more about what we do at atmospherepress.com.

We encourage you to check out some of Atmosphere's latest releases, which are available at Amazon.com and via order from your local bookstore:

Dancing with David, a novel by Siegfried Johnson

The Friendship Quilts, a novel by June Calender

My Significant Nobody, a novel by Stevie D. Parker

Nine Days, a novel by Judy Lannon

Shining New Testament: The Cloning of Jay Christ, a novel by Cliff Williamson

Shadows of Robyst, a novel by K. E. Maroudas

Home Within a Landscape, a novel by Alexey L. Kovalev

Motherhood, a novel by Siamak Vakili

Death, The Pharmacist, a novel by D. Ike Horst

Mystery of the Lost Years, a novel by Bobby J. Bixler

Bone Deep Bonds, a novel by B. G. Arnold

Terriers in the Jungle, a novel by Georja Umano

Into the Emerald Dream, a novel by Autumn Allen

His Name Was Ellis, a novel by Joseph Libonati

The Cup, a novel by D. P. Hardwick

The Empathy Academy, a novel by Dustin Grinnell

Tholocco's Wake, a novel by W. W. VanOverbeke

Dying to Live, a novel by Barbara Macpherson Reyelts

Looking for Lawson, a novel by Mark Kirby

Surrogate Colony, a novel by Boshra Rasti

ABOUT THE AUTHOR

Matt Edwards, author of *Ways and Truths and Lives*, was born and raised in Boise, Idaho, formerly the Northwest's best kept secret, where he developed an affinity for literature: both the challenge of understanding it and the potential to be understood through it. This propelled Matt to study English at Boise State University and devote himself to teaching high school English in the Boise area since 2006. Matt now enjoys sharing his life of passions with his wife and their one and only son. In his free time, if Matt's not training for marathons, he's writing fiction and poetry, mostly about gods and fathers and good, strong drinks.

Made in the USA
Monee, IL
20 November 2023

46948462R00094